DECK

...The Balls

DL GALLIE

It's going to be a nutty Christmas.

Published by DL Gallie Author 2021 (c)

First published in Christmas Treats 1 November 2020

Re-published 30 November 2021

Edited by Karen Hrdlicka, Barren Acres Editing

Proofread by Margaret Neal

Cover Design © Designed with Grace

Image © DepositPhotos – csakisti

Formatting by DL Gallie

INGREDIENTS

One sassy woman—Reese Turner

One stubborn man—Jesse Thornton

A Christmas baking competition

METHOD

1. Throw woman and man together

2. Combine with teasing and taunting

3. Simmer with sexual chemistry

4. Add alcohol to loosen the lips

5. Mix and see what happens

It's going to be a nutty Christmas

ALSO BY DL GALLIE

STAND ALONES

Out of Nowhere

Antecedent

Doc Steel

Oops

Off the Books

Fractured:A driven world novel

Deck...the Balls

I Pucking Hate That I Love You - coming Jan 2022

Seven Nights

Seven Kisses - coming Dec 2021

In the Dark of Night anthology**

Secrets anthology**

**only available in paperback direct from me*

FALLING NOVELS

Falling for Dr. Kelly

Falling for Dr. Knight

Falling for Agent Cox

Falling for Agent Cruz

Falling: The Complete Collection

THE UNEXPECTED SERIES

When it comes to love, expect the unexpected

The Unexpected Gift

The Unexpected Letter

The Unexpected Package

The Unexpected Connection

The Unexpected series: The Complete Collection

THE CASTAWAY GROVE COLLECTION

Love has arrived in the Grove

Oasis

Unequivocal Love

Five Words

Broken Rules

...and a few more to come.

The Castaway Grove Collection, Vol 1

THE LIQUOR CABINET SERIES

Liquor has never been so disturbingly saucy

Malt Me (Book 1)

Tequila Healing (Book 2)

Wine Not (Book 3)

The Final Shot (Book 4)

The Liquor Cabinet: Series boxset

Stefanie,
You claimed Jesse, he's officially all yours...I won't tell
*Marshall **wink wink***

...senior year, high school

"SHORT STACK, YOU GONNA ASK SANTA FOR A LITTLE extra height this Christmas?" Jesse Thornton taunts me from behind in the cafeteria line.

Clenching my jaw, I take a deep breath. I open my mouth to berate him when my best friend, Drew Jacobson, turns to face the stupid jackass. "And maybe you should ask Santa for manners." She grabs my arm and pulls me along the lunch line, pushing a few juniors out of the way to get us away from my nemesis.

"Gah, he's such a jackass. I hate him so much," I scoff, resting my head on my bestie's arm while we wait for the line to move. "Why does he taunt me?" I whine, as I hand my tray to lunch lady Norma and she slops what's meant to be mac 'n cheese on my plate. I eye the fluorescent yellow concoction and swallow back the lump forming in the back of my throat. Like seriously, how can you fuck up mac 'n cheese? And even more so, how do you fuck it up when it comes from a freakin' box?

"You know what they say?" she says, handing over her tray. "Boys tease girls whom they like."

"Pfft, you're full of shit, Drew Jacobson. Jesse Thornton hates me just as much as you hate mushrooms."

"Mushrooms ARE gross and there is no denying that. Those little fungy F'ers can F right back to the dirt where they came from."

"You're hatred for them is getting stronger as the years pass."

"NEVER will I like them. Never, ever ever." She pauses for effect. "N-E-V-E-R." Drew's hatred for mushies is strong, much like my dislike of Jesse Thornton.

"Never say never," I sass back.

Drew eyes me and then smirks. "Never say never also works for you too, Reese Turner. One of these days, you and Jesse Thornton are going to fall madly in love. Mark my word."

"Yeah, and you'll like mushrooms and the Buffalo Bills will win the Super Bowl."

We both laugh because hell will freeze over before Drew will ever like mushies and unless Brady joins Buffalo Bills, they will never win a Super Bowl.

We make our way over to our table and sit down. "I can assure you one million percent that Jesse and I are never gonna happen," I firmly say with a shrug and to reiterate my point, I say it again. "N-E-V-E-R, and stop using our full names, it's weird."

"Nev—"

Lifting my hand, I cover her mouth. "This conversation is over. The end. Done. Not gonna happen. So let's drop it and get back to, eating whatever the hell this is meant to be."

The bitch licks my palm and I pull it away, sliding it down the sleeve of her sweater. Sticking out my tongue at her, I pick up my fork and look down at what's meant to be mac 'n cheese, I shudder and throw my fork down in disgust, but it bounces off my plate and onto the floor—see, even my fork wants to get away from the slop.

Sighing, I lean to the side to pick it up and my head collides with something hard. The hardness growls in agony and when I look up, I realize that my head collided with Jesse's—

"—balls," he groans in pain.

Across from me, Drew is laughing...as is the rest of the cafeteria. All of our fellow students are in stitches laughing at me decking Jesse in the balls. I'm in shock and Jesse, well, he's in pain.

"You just decked him in the balls," someone yells out, stating the obvious and this causes a few students to now cackle with laughter.

"No fucking shit," Jesse snarls through clenched teeth. He's still bent over, cupping said balls in his hands.

"Ohh My God, I'm so sorry," I quickly spit out in one breath. "I didn't see you. I was just picking up my fork and then my head and your balls. Shitballs." My eyes widen when I realize I said balls. "Crapballs," I groan, once again, I said the word balls. "Shit, Oh My God, shoot me now." I ramble, "Crap, just stop talking, Reese. Just apologize and we can move on." Lifting my gaze to Jesse, I finally get my apology out. "I'm so sorry, Jesse."

"You're cute when you waffle," he says, his tone endearing and it totally takes me by surprise. "But it's fine." He says fine through clenched teeth. "I'll catch ya later," he adds before turning around and walking back over to his table.

"That was gold," Drew says, wiping the tears from her eyes.

"Do you think that really hurt?" I ask her, my eyes locked on Jesse as he makes his way back over to his table with the rest of the cool kids.

She nods. "Uhh, huh. When you hit your vag bone, does it hurt?" I nod at her. "There's your answer. Maybe you should go over and rub them better?"

"I think I've done enough damage, I'll leave Jesse and his balls alone."

"Maybe it's your chance to swoop in and get your man," she teases.

"Maybe it's time for you to shut it and eat your slop."

She looks down. "I think I'd rather eat mushrooms."

We both laugh.

Grabbing our trays, we dump our uneaten slop, aka mac 'n cheese, in the trash and walk to the exit, heading for home economics. It's my favorite class because I love baking. Not to brag but I make a kick-ass brownie and come Christmas time, I make the best chocolate balls in three counties.

Glancing back over my shoulder, my eyes lock with

Jesse's. He's staring intently at me. My skin heats and from the intensity of his gaze, I begin to wonder if there's any truth to what Drew thinks. Is he mean because he likes me? Or is he just a huge jackass?

"Later, Short Stack," he shouts across the cafeteria.

And those three words confirm it, he's a jackass.

"Dude, she just nailed your nuts," Ryan Stott, my best friend, states, scrunching his face up in hurt, as I fall into the seat next to him. Wincing when my ass hits the chair because my nuts are a little—and by little, I mean a freakin' lot—tender right now.

"Yep, she sure did," I reply.

Ryan's chatting about the upcoming football game but I'm not really listening. My eyes are locked on Reese Turner's and even though I should be pissed the fuck off right now, I'm not. There's something about her that intrigues me. I've always been fascinated by her. She's a do-gooder. A square bear. Quiet. A nerd, a sexy as fuck nerd. She's the total opposite of me. Sure, I'm also an honors student but I'm outgoing. Captain of the football team. The big man on campus. We're total opposites and for some reason, she hates me with a passion. Maybe she and I just need a hate fuck to get over the issues.

"—what do you say?" Ryan's question snaps my attention back to him.

Staring at my best friend, I look at him confused. "Huh?"

He eyes me suspiciously but shakes his head and repeats his questions. "I said, you wanna head to the lake this weekend?"

"Sure, got nothing better to do."

"Wow, feel the love there, bro." I shrug at him, garnering myself a punch to the arm…at least it wasn't my nuts. "Anyway, since the rents will be away, should we invite a few ladies?" He raises his eyebrows at me, dirty fucking dog that he is. He's such a player and even with his wham-bam-thank-you-ma'am reputation, the ladies still line up.

My mind drifts to Reese, this could be my last chance to get her to admit her feelings for me before school finishes in a few weeks and we go to separate colleges. I know that underneath all the contempt for me, she wants me just as much as I want her. There's no way in hell that she'd come on her own and then it hits me. "How about a party instead?" I suggest. "One last hurrah before we head into finals?"

"I like your style, Thornton. I like your style." He offers me his fist and we fist bump. He then pushes his chair back and stands on top of it. "Hear ye, hear ye," he shouts to the room with his hands wrapped around his mouth. "Par-tay this weekend at my lake house. One last hurrah before we begin finals. Come one, come all."

The entire cafeteria erupts into a chorus of cheers. I glance back over to where Reese was, but she's gone. I need to make sure she attends this weekend because this weekend, I will win her over before school finishes. My only goal for this weekend is to win Reese Turner over and get her onto Team Jesse.

Game on Reese, game on.

"I CAN'T BELIEVE YOU CONVINCED ME TO COME TO this party, Drew. Ryan doesn't even know I exist and you and I both know that Jackass Thornton is going to taunt me, like usual." At the beginning of the year he started referring to me as Short Stack—I hate that nickname, just as much as I hate him—and it's stuck. All the guys on the football team call me that now and I can only hope when I go off to college, that name stays here.

"Ohh stop it," Drew berates me. "Everyone knows our valedictorian, you need to give yourself more credit."

"So what you're saying is everyone knows me as the short-stack valedictorian nerd."

"Pretty much," she nonchalantly replies with a shrug. "Look, Reese, babe, it's a party. Let loose for one night and have fun. We're only seniors once."

"What about seniors in college?"

She rolls her eyes at me. "You know what I mean. For

once in your nerdy little life, have fun. Let your inner party animal out, I know she's in there because I have seen you let loose."

"It's easy to do when it's just us."

"So pretend it's just us." A laugh breaks free because it's far from just us, it looks like everyone in our senior year is here. Mind you, it's a Ryan Stott party. Anyone who is someone will be here. "Okay, well yeah, maybe that might be hard to imagine since there's already a billion people here and it's not even nine but, Reese, babe, just have fun."

"Fine," I relent, "but you better not leave my side."

"I promise to stick to your side like glue." But as soon as we walk through the front doors, I know that she will not be by my side for long. From across the room, Russell "Rusty" Richards is eye-fucking her, and she is returning said eye-fucking.

Drew has been lusting over Rusty since the third grade—and yes, his name really is Russell Richards, hence why he goes by Rusty most of the time. My bestie has always thought he was out of her league, but blind Freddie can see that the two of them have a connection. And as I stand here and watch the two of them, I'm going to make sure that tonight, my best friend gets her man. If anyone deserves to be happy, it's my bestie...even if she is lusting over a dude named Russell "Rusty" Richards.

"Come on," I link my arm with her, "let's grab a drink." And I start walking over to where Rusty is.

"What have you done with my best friend?" she teases as we weave in between partygoers. "You are willingly walking into this party, what gives?"

Shrugging my shoulders, we stop before Rusty. "Hey, Rusty," I say in greeting.

"Reese. Drew," he replies, and from beside me, I feel my best friend shiver at the sound of his voice. "Can I get you ladies a drink?"

I wait for Drew to reply but she's frozen and mute, a first for her. "Sure," I say, breaking the silence. "Coke for me since I'm DD and a vodka cranberry for Drew."

"Coming right up." He walks away from us and heads into the kitchen, Drew turns her head to me and mouths, 'what the fuck.' I just shrug, feigning ignorance.

A few moments later, Rusty returns with our drinks. "Here you go."

"Thanks," I reply, taking my red Solo cup from him. "Ahhhhhhhh that's…I'll be right back," and I quickly walk away, leaving my best friend with the man of her dreams. Before I step outside, I look over my shoulder and a smile graces my face at seeing my bestie pulling on her big girl panties and chatting to Rusty. "Get your man, girl," I whisper but my smile soon disappears when from the corner of my eye, I see *him*.

Walking across the patio, I look up and see the one person I was hoping to avoid leaning against the railing. "Short Stack, you made it," he greets and from beside him, Ryan snorts at his friend's greeting.

"Not drinking tonight?" Ryan asks me as I join them, my feet taking me over to them even though I'd rather be anywhere but here with them.

"Nope, I'm DD," I tell him, lifting my Coke and taking a sip.

"No surprises that the square bear isn't drinking," he teases.

"Well, I think it's great," Jesse interjects, shocking me that he's sticking up for me. "Drew's lucky to have a good friend like you, but I think you might be driving home alone tonight." He points over my shoulder. Turning my head, I smile when I see Drew and Rusty have ventured out here, and the two of them are making out against the side of the house.

"That didn't take long," I mumble to myself with a grin.

"What didn't take long?" Jesse questions.

"Them two." I head nod to Drew and Rusty.

"For them to start making out?"

Shaking my head, I look back to Jesse. "No, for them to get together."

"Weren't they already?"

"Nope."

"Wow, I always thought they were a couple. The chemistry between the two of them is off the charts."

"I know, right? Seems everyone but the two of them could see that, but it looks like finally they've realized it too. Drew has been lusting over him since the third grade but she never tried because she always thought she'd have zero chance with him, but—"

Jesse laughs and it pisses me off. "Something funny, jackass?" I snarl at him.

"You're cute when you waffle, Short Stack."

"I don't waffle." I retort, then I add, "and don't call me cute...or Short Stack."

"Just stating a fact," he says with a shrug, and there's

not an ounce of jest on his face or in his tone. He's serious about me being cute.

A silence forms between us, until Ryan says, "Another pair who just needs to give in." His statement garners himself a slap up the side of his head from Jesse.

"And on that note, I need more beer." He pushes off the railing and heads inside, shouting, "It's shot time!"

Neither Jesse or I say anything, we silently stand here and watch everyone race back inside to do shots with Ryan. I wish I had no fear like him but instead, I awkwardly stand here with Jesse, neither one of us saying a word. Then my brain registers what Ryan said before he went inside. *Another pair who just needs to give in.*

What the hell did he mean by that? Surely he's not referring to Jesse and me? He hates my guts, and me, well, I don't exactly know how I feel about him.

Leaning against the railing, I look to the house next door and smile.

"What's with the smile?" he asks me.

"I love the house next door, I always have. One day, I'd love to own it."

Jesse just nods at my statement but doesn't say anything. He leans against the railing next to me and stares out at the lake. Watching him from the corner of my eye, I take the moment to appreciate him. He really is good-looking, it's a shame he's such a dick.

"Come again?" he growls with a shocked look on his face...ohh shit, I said that out loud.

"Come again?" I growl and from the wide-eyed, deer caught in the headlights look on her face right now, she didn't mean to say that out loud. "Did you just say I'm a dick?"

"If the dick fits," she snarls, and then her eyes widen farther when she realizes what she just said.

"Trust me, babe, the dick will fit and it will fit you like no dick has ever fit you before."

Her mouth opens and closes. Seems she's stumped for words, this must be a first for Short Stack. She always has a witty comeback and it's one of the things I love most about her. For a pint-sized lil' thang, she sure has a wicked tongue. My eyes drop to her mouth and now I'm picturing what she could do with those lips and her tongue.

A force takes over my body and I step into her. Gripping the back of her neck, I pull her to me. She lifts her head and stares up at me, the anger from before is no longer reflecting in her eyes. She's feeling what I'm feeling. I lower my head down and slam my lips to hers. I kiss her like she's never been kissed before. She's frozen for a few seconds and then she's kissing me back. My tongue slips in and out of her mouth. She nips my lip and pulls back.

We breathlessly stare at one another.

She lifts to her tippy-toes, slips her arms over my shoulders and presses her lips to mine again. This kiss is much slower but it holds just as much passion as our friends' one from a few moments ago.

Sliding my hands down her back, I squeeze her ass and lift her up. Spinning around, I place her on the deck railing so we are at an even height now. Making it easier for us to kiss due to the massive height difference between us.

Our lips never separate.

She runs her hands up the back of my neck and gently pulls on my hair. "I knew you'd like it rough," I murmur against her lips.

"You know nothing, Jesse Thornton."

Resting my forehead against hers, I stare into her eyes. Up close they are more blue than gray, but color aside, they are gorgeous…just like her. "Short Stack, I know that if I slipped my hand inside your pants right now, your cunt would be dripping."

"Don't say the 'c' word, it's crass and disgusting." She slaps me in the chest, pushing me slightly away from her but my hands still grip her sides. I'm the only thing preventing her from falling backward.

"Okay," I try again, "I bet if I slipped my hand inside your pants right now, your lady garden would be dripping."

She slaps me again and snorts a laugh. "Lady garden, really?"

"If you'd just accepted that I said cu—"

She presses her finger to my lips. "Less crass talk, Thornton, more kissing."

"Yes, ma'am," I reply, before covering her mouth with mine again.

Kissing Reese Turner is everything and more. I've kissed a few girls but never has a kiss felt this good. I can feel her kiss deep in my soul, it's etching its name on my heart, forever branding my heart hers.

I'm addicted and if I never kiss anyone again, I'd be okay with it.

———

After my epic make-out session with Reese, which by the way will go down as the best make-out session in the history of make-out sessions, the two of us walk down to the lake. I sling my arm over her shoulder and she slides hers behind me and into the back pocket of my jeans.

"You're the perfect height for this," I tell her.

"Are you calling me short...again?"

"If the short tag fits," I cheekily reply.

"Lucky you're cute," she says, poking me in the stomach, causing me to yelp and flinch.

"So you think I'm cute, hey?" I retort.

"You know you are."

"I wouldn't call myself cute, I'd more say…"

"Say what?"

"Handsome. Dashing. Sexy. Spunky monkey."

"Someone is high on themselves."

"Just stating the truth."

"Modest much?" I just shrug and stare down at her as we continue to walk toward the lake.

It's a full moon tonight, its brightness lights up the night sky as if we are under the floodlights at the stadium. I can see her looking at me sideways. Placing my finger under her chin, I lift her gaze to mine, her eyes sparkling in the moonlight. We stare at one another for a few beats, then I lower my head down and kiss her again.

Turning to face each other, we wrap our arms around one another. Holding each other tightly as we kiss under the big oak tree at the shore.

Walking her backward, I press her up against a tree trunk on the border of the Stott and Reynolds properties, my body cocoons hers. Trapping her between the tree and me. Cupping her breast over her shirt, she moans into our kiss. Tweaking her nipple, her moans increase.

My cock hardens in my jeans, painfully pressing against my zipper.

Pulling back, I stare down at her. Even in the darkness, I can see her cheeks are flushed and her lips swollen. "As much as I'm loving kissing you, Short Stack, if we keep kissing like this, my dick is going to bust through my jeans."

"Ohh," she whispers. Then she shocks me with what she says next, "I can always help you with that."

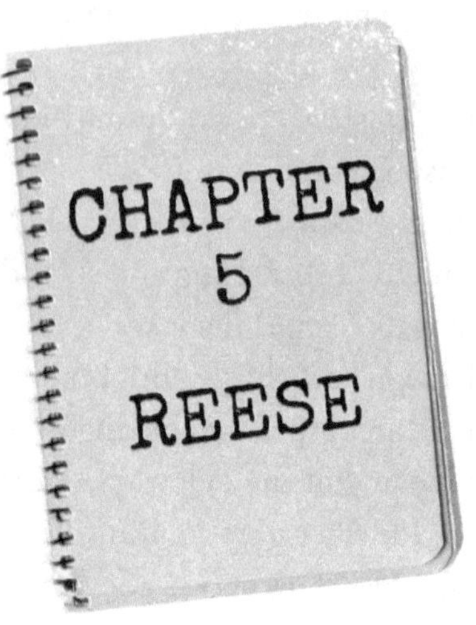

I can always help you with that.

What the hell, Reese?

You don't say things like that. Hell, you don't randomly kiss boys either, especially boys who have relentlessly teased you since the fifth grade, but tonight you seem to be doing a lot of things you normally wouldn't.

I'm seeing Jesse in a completely different light. And it's making me feel different too. I don't know how I feel about it but what I do know is, I don't want to stop kissing him, that man knows how to kiss. I can only imagine what else he knows how to do.

"Yeah, and how can you help with that?" he questions me, the deep timbre of his voice causes me to shiver.

Suddenly I'm shy. "Ummm, ahh, you know." I drop my gaze to the ground and I focus on the grass and my feet.

"I know lots of things but, Reese." He places his finger under my chin and lifts my head so I'm staring up at him. "I need you to TELL me how you can help with this?" To emphasize this, he removes his finger from my chin and cups his junk. My gaze drops to his hand and then back up to his face, the cocky jackass winks at me.

That's all I need. It's like someone has overtaken my body because I step toward him, push his hand out of the way, and I squeeze his junk in my hand. I gently massage his cock through his jeans. "Something like this," I purr, yes I purr.

"That's very good help," he replies, groaning in delight. Hearing him let go has my clit throbbing. Biting my lip, I continue to stare up at him while I palm and stroke his cock. Pulling my hand away, he groans in frustration, until he realizes that I'm flicking open the button on his jeans. "You really don't have to," he huskily says, his gaze locked on mine.

"I want to," I honestly tell him and it's the honest to God truth. I want to do this for him. For me. For some inexplicable reason, I just need to.

Dropping to my knees, my eyes are locked on his as I lower his fly. Licking my bottom lip, I bite it. He cups the side of my face and with the pad of his thumb, he pulls my lip free. "I fucking love it when you bite your lip like that."

I smile up at him, I'm about to slip my hand into his briefs when from nearby, someone squeals and then there's a splash, followed by giggles and another splash.

From my spot down on my knees, I stare up at him,

wide-eyed. Wondering if now that we have an audience I should stop.

I'm not sure what to do.

To be honest, I think I'm relieved we were interrupted, but there's also a part of me that's upset. I'm loving this change in the dynamic between Jesse and me but as I stare up at him, I realize I don't want my first blow job to be in such a public arena.

Standing up, Jesse growls in frustration but then he cups my cheek and stares intently at me. I don't see hate or animosity reflecting back, I see admiration and lust, but that's probably because I was about to suck his dick. "You head on up, I'll fix this," he points to his junk, "and then I'll find you."

"Okay," I reply, my shyness has returned.

Stepping to the side, I go to walk around him when he grabs my wrist, pulls me, and presses my back into the tree trunk. Before I can process what's happening, his lips are on mine once again. Our tongues seductively twining together in an erotic dance. This kiss trumps the other kisses and those kisses were everything.

"I love kissing you," he pants against my lips.

"I love kissing you too but us kissing more won't help."

"Help with what?"

"This," I state, cupping his still hard cock in my hand.

"It's worth it." He slams his lips back to mine and I continue to rub his cock.

"Fuuuuck," he moans against my lips. "I really need you to stop, Reese, or I'm gonna make a mess."

"Do you really want me to?" I sassily reply,

wondering where this sexy vixen version of me is coming from.

"Yes," he snaps, before growling through clenched teeth, "No."

Feeling brave, I slip my hand inside his open pants and under his briefs. I grip his cock in my palm and squeeze his shaft tight. He groans into our kiss as I begin to stroke him. I've never done this before but thanks to Drew making me watch my first porn the other week, I have a vague idea on what to do.

Flicking my wrist back and forth, I slide my hand up and down his shaft. It's tight within the confines of his jeans and briefs, but I must be doing it right because from the moans coming from Jesse, he seems to be enjoying himself.

His lips are still locked to mine as I continue to stroke his cock. His body freezes and he grunts into my mouth as I feel a warm liquid coat my hand.

Jesse breaks our kiss and stares at me. "Fuuuuck, I... umm, I, just wow." He's mumbling incoherently, like his brain is fried. Pulling my hand out of his pants, I step back from him. He reaches out, grips my wrist, and wipes my hand with his shirt.

"Jesse—" He presses his finger to my lips, silencing me.

"Reese, you don't need to say a thing. That was single-handedly the most erotic experience of my life." He pauses. "Do you want me to return the favor?"

Do I? I question myself silently and I find myself nodding before I can think about it further. A grin lights up his face and once again, he backs me into the trunk of the tree. He leans one arm next to my head and stares down at me. He glides his hand down my side, it tickles and I giggle. Slipping his hand between my legs, he begins to trace up my inner thigh and under my skirt. Goose pimples appear. My body thrums. He reaches my panties and runs the tip of his finger ever so lightly over my mound.

My eyes droop closed and I moan at the sensation. I've touched myself a few times like this before but when it's someone else, it's so much more intense.

"Eyes on me, Short Stack," he growls.

My eyes open and I stare up at him. His eyes are locked on mine as he pushes my panties to the slide and without warning presses his finger inside. My eyes widen and I moan.

"Fuck, Reese, you're so wet," he whispers. "Did jerking me off turn you on?"

Nodding my head, I stare at him as he continues to thrust his finger in and out. "Kiss me," I breathlessly pant.

He stares at me for a few seconds and then he lowers his head. He covers my mouth with his. His tongue slips in and out in sync with his fingers in my pussy.

My body is buzzing.

I've never felt like this before. I moan into the kiss and begin to gyrate my hips against his hand. "Jesse," I pant, "I'm close."

He presses his thumb against my clit and I explode. My eyes close and fireworks erupt throughout my body and I scream into his kiss.

I'm breathing deeply, he pulls his fingers out and lifts them to his lips and sucks. He licks my climax off his fingers and moans in delight. "Fuck, Reese, you taste like heaven."

Gripping his cheeks in my palms, I press my lips to his. I can taste myself on his lips; it's tart, not what I expected but then again, I've never really thought about what I taste like.

Breaking the kiss, we stare at one another. The air around us zinging and pinging. It would be the perfect moment to lose my 'V' card but the moment is interrupted when Ryan yells out, "Yo, Jesse, you out here?"

"Fuck," Jesse snarls. "Be right there," he yells back to Ryan.

"Wanna move this back to the party?" he asks me, nodding my head, I smile.

We each readjust our clothing and head back to the party. When we get inside, I head to the bathroom to wash up. I pass the den and see Drew and Rusty making out. A smile graces my face, I'm so happy my best friend got her man, finally.

Using the restroom, I wash up and head out in search of Jesse. I'm just about to step into the kitchen when I hear Ryan.

"What's going on with you and nerd girl?"

"It's nothing," I overhear Jesse tell Ryan and that hurts. Then he shoves the knife in deeper the longer I listen to him and Ryan.

"You were kissing Reese….and more. What gives with you and Short Stack?"

"It was nothing, just forget it."

"Totally looked like more to me, do you like her or something?"

My eyes widen and I hold my breath, waiting for his answer. "No—"

One word.

Two letters.

And my entire world crashes down at my feet.

I knew he was an asshole, but this, this is a new low, even for him. I don't wait to hear what else he says, I turn on my heel and leave. I race toward my car, ever so grateful that I'm driving.

Climbing into the driver's seat, the first tear falls. Leaning my head on the steering wheel, I let the tears flow. Thank God I didn't go all the way with him, I can only imagine what he'd say then. "Asshole," I tearfully mumble.

Putting the key into the ignition, I start my car, I'm just about to pull out and then I remember Drew. Pulling my phone out, I shoot her a text.

REESE: *Heading home, not feeling well. Sorry Xo*
REESE: *PS. Jesse is a dick*

I'm not expecting to get a reply because the last I saw, Drew and Rusty were sucking face but to my surprise, I get a reply.

DREW: *I knew that, hope you're ok. I'll call you tomorrow*
REESE: *You better, I want to hear all about you and your man. Enjoy your night with Rusty **wink wink***
DREW: *He's everything and more. Love your face*

REESE: *Love your face too...use protection **wink wink***

DREW: *Reese Turner, what kind of girl do you take me for???*

DREW: *And of course I will...I'm an angel **angel emoji***

I snort a laugh at the message. Drew and angel do not go together in a sentence, or even the same room, but if anyone deserves to be happy, it's my best friend. Even if I'm heartbroken right now, I can be happy for her. That's what friends do.

REESE: *More like a fallen angel*

REESE: *But seriously, have fun and be safe. Chat tomorrow*

DREW: ***laughing emoji** **middle finger emoji***

REESE: ***kiss face emoji***

DREW: ***kiss face emoji***

Throwing my phone into the cupholder, I pull out onto the road and head home. As I drive past Ryan's house, I see Jesse running down the driveway. Our eyes lock when I drive by. He looks confused and starts racing down the driveway, I put my foot down and hightail it out of there. I don't need to be embarrassed any more.

Pulling into the garage at home, I grab my things and press the button to lower the door. I quietly head inside and find Dad asleep in the recliner. The TV is on, the light reflecting on him. Grabbing the blanket off the sofa,

I drape it over him. Kissing him on the forehead, I whisper, "Night, Daddy." And then I head up to my room.

Walking into my bathroom, I flick on the light and look at my reflection. My lips are swollen and my cheeks are still a little flushed. Running my index finger over my lips, I remember the feel of his lips against mine. My eyes well with tears, I cover my mouth and suck a deep breath in. As I inhale, I smell his release still on my hand and the first tear falls as I think about tonight. I went from a massive high, to a massive low. All thanks to Jesse-fucking-Thornton. How am I going to get through the last few weeks of school now?

After heading back inside, Reese uses the restroom and I head to the kitchen to grab us fresh drinks. I've just popped the cap on a beer when Ryan waltzes over to me. "What gives with you and Short Stack?"

Normally I'm one to boast about my hookups but with Short Stack, I want to keep what happened between us and us only. "None of your fucking business, now drop it before I drop you." I try and deflect him but Ryan is like a dog with a bone.

"Wow, chill the fuck out, dude. It was just a question."

"And I told you it's nothing." *Nothing I want to discuss with you anyway.* "Now, we going to play beer pong or what?"

"So you wanna get your ass whipped, do you?" Ryan throws back at me.

"You've got that the wrong way around, asshole. You get it set up, I'm gonna take a piss and then I'll come back and whip your ass."

He flips me the bird. I chug back the rest of my beer and then I head to the bathroom. Surprisingly, it's empty. I take a piss and wash my hands. Exiting into the hallway, I see Drew coming toward me. She and Rusty have finally given into their desires and hooked up, I look behind them, hoping to see Short Stack but she's not there.

My gaze flicks back to Drew and she's fuming. By the looks of things, her anger is directed at me. "You really are a dick," she growls, angrily poking me in the chest. "Why must you do that to her?"

"Do what?" I question, completely confused right now.

"As if you don't know. Just, ugh, fuck you, Thornton." She looks to Rusty, and her face is now all angelic like and sweet. "Can you drop me home since Reese left?"

"She left?" Hearing that hurts, she left without saying goodbye.

"Not that it's any of your business, but yes she did cause you—" Not waiting to hear what else she has to say, I race down the hallway and out through the front doors. I head down the driveway and hear a car. Picking up my speed, I look up just as Reece's dad's red Jeep passes by. Our eyes lock as she rolls past. It looks like she's crying, it cuts me that she's upset and I hate seeing her like that. Racing down the driveway, I yell out, "Reese, wait up!" But she puts her foot down on the accelerator and speeds away. Leaving me confused at her about-face just now.

Dejectedly, I walk back up the driveway and into the house. Drew gives me the evil eye and I make my way into the kitchen where Ryan is playing beer pong against Leigh Levelly, and from the fuck me eyes they're giving each other, I give them three minutes before he takes her upstairs to his bedroom.

Well, look at that, it was three seconds and not three minutes. He claps me on the shoulder and winks as he drags her up to his room. Wolf whistles and cheers follow them as they go.

Grabbing another beer, I twist the cap off and head back out to the deck. Leaning on the rail, I look down to the water's edge and my eyes land on the tree where Reese and I had our moment earlier. And then I think about her leaving and the sad look in her eyes as she drove way. "What was that all about?" I whisper to myself.

Guess I'll find out on Monday at school...but I never find out what happened. For the rest of the school year, all three weeks, Reese avoids me like the plague. Drew plays interference and always keeps me away, never allowing me to get answers to my questions.

Graduation day arrives and still, it's radio silent from Reese. She beats me for valedictorian but if I have to lose —only by a few points—to anyone, I'm glad it is to her. She looks amazing up on stage giving her speech. I was hoping to have a chance to talk to her afterward but once again, Drew plays interference and I don't get my chance to speak to her.

"Drew, please tell me what I've done?" I beg.

"If you don't know, then you're a bigger jackass than I

ever gave you credit before. Just leave her alone, Jesse. You've done enough damage." And with that, she turns on her heel and leaves me standing here stunned. What the hell did I do? But more importantly, why do I care so much that she's ignoring me?

...current day

MEN SUCK. THEY CAN ALL GO EAT A BAG OF BIG FAT hairy dicks, especially Quintin Marquis and his hobag slut face, Jennifer Collins. I knew I didn't like the bitch, she's Quintin's assistant, and apparently his side piece too. She always rubbed me the wrong way and it seems she was also rubbing him.

Today's staff meeting wrapped up much quicker than expected, thank God 'cause it's Friday. *Who puts a meeting on a Friday afternoon?* I was already in a mood after the last-minute meeting and that mood increased when I arrive home.

Opening the front door, I walk into the apartment I share with Quintin, I find my loving douchebag boyfriend with his face between his assistant's legs, eating her out on the sofa, my new sofa that I just bought.

And to add salt into the wound, when he sees me standing here, he continues to dine on his ho. With his eyes locked on mine, the jerkface asshole brings her to climax. Once she's finished riding his face, he lifts his head up and smiles at me. His chin coated in her juices.

"What the fuck?" I snarl, that garners Jennifer's attention and in slow motion, I watch as she jumps up in fright. She trips on her feet and falls, hitting her head on the coffee table, busting her forehead open. Blood sprays my new sofa—grrrrr—and all over Quintin. His face pales at the sight of the blood and he passes out, landing on the sofa. Looking like Sleeping Beauty in his passed out state.

Me being me, I race into the kitchen, grab the first aid kit and I attend to my boyfriend's skank's bleeding head. Once she's patched up, she hightails it out of our apartment, leaving me with a passed-out boyfriend, a blood-spattered sofa, and a broken heart.

Walking into the kitchen, I throw the first aid kit on the counter and drop the dressings into the trash. Leaning against the counter, I close my eyes and sigh. My eyes well with tears. I'm sad, hurt, and broken-hearted right now. I love Quintin with all my heart and this is how he repays that love. Men fucking suck.

Grabbing a glass of water, I chug it back and just as I place the empty glass down, Quintin shuffles into the kitchen. "Babe, I'm—"

"Save it, Quintin. I don't want to hear your excuses. You should have had the decency to break up with me before you moved on." He looks to the floor and I realize that this has obviously been going on for a while. "How long?" I growl.

"Ummm…"

"Just tell me," I demand.

"Since spring break."

"What the hell, Quintin? Why? What could I have possibly done to deserve this?"

"Nothing, you're perfect in every way."

"If I'm so perfect, why cheat?"

"I…I don't know. I'm just…shit…"

"You know what, save it. I don't want to hear your lies. I'm going to Drew's for a few days to nurse my broken heart. There's no coming back from this, Q. We're over. Done. Dusted. Kaput. You've broken my trust and heart. Don't be here when I get back."

Not letting him get a word in, I push past him. Racing into our bedroom, with tears in my eyes, I pack a bag. Walking back out, I find Q in the same spot, he hasn't moved. I exit our apartment and drive straight over to Drew and Rusty's place. I park Betty in the driveway and walk up the front path, I'm about to knock on the door when from the porch swing, Drew coos, "What's up, Buttercup?"

Jumping in fright, I drop my bag and cover my chest with my hand. "Shit, I didn't see you there."

Walking over, I plonk down next to her, rest my head on her shoulder, and sigh. "What's got you down?"

"I just walked in on Q going to town on his assistant's snatch. The asshole stared at me as she climaxed and then when I announced my presence, she tripped, busted her forehead open on the coffee table, getting blood all over my new sofa, Quintin, the pansy, passed out. I fixed up her head, she left. We broke up and now I'm here."

"Holy fuck," Drew drawls, and then scrunches her face, "You attended to Q's skank's busted head while he was passed out on the sofa?"

"Yep," I reply, letting the 'p' pop.

"You're too nice, Reese. I hope you were rough with the ho."

"No," I whisper. Lifting my head up, I look to Drew and my eyes well with tears. "He was cheating on me," I cry, the first tear falls and then an avalanche follows. "Why did he cheat? Am I a shitty lay? Why?" Drew pulls me into her arms and I sob my broken heart out. "What did I do to deserve this? Men suck donkeydick."

"Ohh, babe," she whispers. "He cheated 'cause he's a douche. I'm sure you're a good lay and as for the why, it's because he's a dick and you're too good for him."

"She got blood on my new sofa," I cry again.

"That's future Reese's problem. Right now Reese, she needs to come inside with me. We're gonna drink wine and watch reality telly. Rusty will pick up Chinese and ice cream, and then tomorrow we'll come up with a game plan."

"Thank God it's Friday," I tell her, "and yes, that sounds like a plan."

Drew and I do exactly that for the next two days. It was the perfect way to deal with my broken heart. On Sunday afternoon, I put on my big girl panties and return to the apartment. When I open the door, I'm once again shocked at what I find.

In the two days I was at Drew's, Quintin, the asshole fuckface dickwad cleaned out our apartment. He took everything, and I mean everything. He left me with nothing but dust and my clothes, thrown in a pile in the middle of our bedroom. The fucker even took my half used toiletries. And to add insult to the wound, he racked up charges on my credit card. Leaving me with an empty apartment, a broken heart, and in debt up to my eyeballs.

Men suck donkeyballs.

...twelve months later

RETURNING TO MY HOMETOWN WASN'T IN THE PLAN but when I was offered the principal position at Willows Grove Elementary, it was too good of an offer to refuse. So here I am, back in Willows Grove. The place I grew up and vowed never to return to, famous last words I guess.

The town hasn't changed much over the years, it's still as picturesque as I remember and the people are just as friendly. Well most of them are, Reese Turner is still an ice queen around me.

I really thought when we hooked up at Ryan's party that that was the turning point for us. I thought we'd turned a corner.

We kissed.

We fondled.

We kissed some more and to date, that night was one of the best nights of my life.

And then it all turned to shit. Our relationship, took a massive nosedive after Ryan's party at the lake and still, to this day, I have no idea why.

If I close my eyes, I can still remember the feel of her hand on my dick as she stroked me. Fuuuuck, and the kisses, fuck me. Those kisses are single-handedly the best kisses of my life.

All these years later, there's one thing that's still the same, she's just as sexy as I remember but she's not the quiet meek girl from school anymore. Now she's a sexy AF little spitfire. Clearly, Drew has rubbed off on her. She was always the outspoken and crazy one, the fact they are best friends always confused me 'cause they're so different.

I nearly fell off my chair when I read over the staff list and saw that I was now her boss. I've stalked her on Facebook over the years, not in a creepy way, just in a 'what's she been up to' way.

She was dating some dude for a while but it looks like they broke up, maybe it's fate's way of giving us the chance we never got in senior year? Maybe it's my chance to get the answer as to why she iced me out.

Running my hand over my face, I lean back in my office chair and wonder what life would have been like if Reese and I got our chance back then. Would we still be together? Married? Kids? The possibilities are endless but it doesn't matter because she hates my guts with a fiery passion. I just hope it doesn't affect our working relationship, I'd hate to have to fire her. I'm sure that would win me brownie points, not. From what I've seen so far and heard, she's an excellent teacher but that doesn't surprise me. She was always nurturing and helping people.

My phone rings and when I look down, I see it's Mom. "Hey, Mom."

"I need you to pick up some mushrooms and wine on your way over tonight."

"Hello to you too, Mom. I'm good, thanks for asking. What's got you in a fluster today?" And before she answers, I know exactly what she's going to say, that's another thing that hasn't changed. Her and Stefanie Arnold's rivalry.

Stefanie Arnold and my mom have had a love/hate relationship for as long as I can remember. No one knows what it started over but it's a rivalry that will go down in history, that's for sure. I wouldn't be surprised if in years to come, there's a chapter in the Willows Grove history books about this.

"Stefanie Arnold cheated at bingo today."

BINGO—pun intended. "Did she cheat? Or are you—"

"She cheated!" Mom yells down the line, "Don't say she didn't, you weren't there."

"Okay. Okay," I placate her. "Now, what did you need me to pick up?" That gets her off the topic of Stefanie Arnold, for now. She's now focused on what's missing for dinner this evening.

"I'm just leaving school now, Mom, I'll pick up those few things and head on over."

"Thank you, Jesse. See you soon."

"Bye, Mom."

Hanging up, I shut my computer down and lock up the office. Walking toward the exit, I pass by Reese's classroom and notice she's still here. "You're working late," I say.

Reese squeals and covers her chest with her hand. "Shit, you scared me," she breathlessly replies and then, when she sees it's me, she scowls.

Leaning against the doorframe, I watch her. "I didn't think anyone else was here."

"Some principal you are," she snaps. "I'm just finalizing a few things for the new curriculum we're starting in a couple weeks." We silently stare at one another. The intensity in her gaze reminds me of that night. Our connection is still there. Maybe she doesn't feel it, but I sure as fuck do, however it's always trumped by her hatred toward me. A hatred that, I don't understand.

"I can lock up when I'm done, you don't need to hang around."

Our eyes are still locked on one another, when her phone rings, interrupting our moment. She dives for it and answers, "Hey, Drew."

She turns her back to me to take the call. That's my cue to leave so I wave goodbye, not that she saw. I turn around, leaving her on the phone with Drew and leaving me confused as hell once again regarding our connection, or whatever the hell it is between us.

Walking around the store, I fill my basket with the things Mom asked me to pick up when all of a sudden, the corner of a shopping cart hits me in the nuts. My eyes widen and I drop the basket. "My balls," I groan, bending over to cover my junk to ease the pain.

Lifting my head up, I see a wide-eyed Reese staring at me. "Ohh shit, are you okay?" she asks, her tone endearing, she really is worried about me and my nuts.

"Fine," I reply through clenched teeth.

"Let me," she says, dropping to her knees. She turns my basket upright and begins to put the things back in. She lifts her head up and I have a déjà vu moment. I'm transported back to that night down by the lake when she was on her knees, offering to give me a blow job. I often wonder if we hadn't been interrupted whether she would have gone through with it.

My eyes drop to her lips and I imagine her lips wrapped around my shaft. It sliding in and out of her mouth. My dick twitches at the thought and from where she's crouching, she has a direct view of my twitching cock.

She rolls her eyes before standing up and handing me my basket. Shaking it angrily into my chest. Before I have a chance to say anything, she grabs her cart, pushes it around me, and storms off.

Sighing, I shake my head and walk toward the cashier. "Jesse," she calls out.

Looking over my shoulder, I reply, "Yeah?"

"Sorry about your balls." She grins and fuck me sideways, it lights her face up. A laugh escapes me when I register what she said. I stand here and watch her walk away, she really has no clue about the hold she has on me, and my balls. Now that I'm back, I hope with everything I have, that one of these days, my balls and I finally get a proper chance with her.

CHAPTER 9
REESE

"And the winner is... Jesse Thornton," Stefanie Arnold, the fair baking superintendent announces.

My mouth drops open, I was beaten by *him*, really? I'm not upset I lost, I'm pissed off I lost to *him*, again. First he takes the job that was meant to be mine and now, he takes first place at the county fair. My brownies are so much better than his snicker-fucking-doodles; it's not hard to bake a shitty cookie and roll it in cinnamon sugar.

"He's such a jackass," I mumble.

"Ohh shit, Reese is pissed," Rusty—my best friend's husband—says from behind his beer mug.

"Well, they were delish," Drew agrees, snuggling into his side, like they always do. I'd vomit at their affection for one another but Drew and Rusty are perfect for each other in every way possible. I'm so glad my matchmaking skills at that lake party in senior year worked, it's a shame that *my* own matchmaking skills that night let me down.

My gaze snaps to Drew when I register that she's agreeing *his* cookies are good, I give her the evil eye. She shrugs her shoulders nonchalantly. "What? They were delish," she protests, my eyes widen farther at her honesty. "Not your brownies good, but still—"

"—good. I get it," I snap at her.

Some best friend she is, I think to myself as I watch everyone congregate around *him*, congratulating *him* on his win. The jackass probably cheated. He probably got his mom to bake them for him. But I know that's not true, Mrs. Thornton is the best pie baker in three counties, her pecan pie is THE best pie ever and she's just sweet as pie too. She wouldn't help her son cheat. It seems like *he* inherited her baking talents, pity he didn't inherit her niceness.

Sitting back in my chair, I cross my arms and huff. My dislike for Jesse Thornton is just as strong as ever, and this defeat is like a knife to the heart. You'd think my dislike for him from high school would have passed over the years but nope, it's still there. Back then, he was your typical jock—hot, popular, and everyone bowed down to him. I fell for his charm that night in senior year and the hot popular jackass jock broke my little heart. I listened to Drew and took heed that he teased me because he liked me. But ohh, how wrong I was.

Thankfully, we went our separate ways after graduation and I never saw him again, until he returned to Willows Grove not that long ago. Even though we went our separate ways, his nickname for me, Short Stack, followed me to college thanks to his best friend, Ryan

Stott, also attending Silver Oak University, damn jackasses.

Life was grand here in Willows Grove without Jesse-freakin'-Thornton but now he's back and he still rubs me the wrong way. It's like high school all over again, but worse because he's hotter than he was back then AND he's my boss.

Boy oh boy, he fills out a dress shirt in the sexiest of sexiest ways and don't get me started on his ass in his slacks. He's still a mega jackass and still refers to me as Short Stack but there's nothing I can do, not if I want to keep my job. He returned as principal of Willows Grove Elementary, that position was mine but no, Jesse-freakin'-Thornton had to once again stomp all over me.

My eyes are locked on *him* and I start to fume even more, not only is he an asshole but he's a sexy as sin asshole. He's always been hot but since returning, it seems he got sexier. Broad shoulders. Muscly arms. The most kissable lips I've ever seen...or felt. *Damn him.* Chocolate brown hair I want to run my fingers through and the bluest of blue eyes you can lose yourself in. They remind me of the Caribbean Sea, and then there's his voice. It's deep and rough but at the same time it's soft and sweet, it vibrates through your body. Each cell and nerve ending coming alive at the sound. His face is covered in a light fuzz that he keeps groomed and occasionally, he lets it grow into a sexy as hell beard. It's a shame his beautiful looks and killer baking skills are the total opposite of his shitty 'I'm a jackass' personality.

He catches me staring at him but I quickly glance away, picking up my drink—a Dark 'N' Stormy. I look around the fair and smile. These fairs are the best part of living here and the people are great too, well most of them. But my most favorite part, is the homemade ginger beer. The homemadeness—that's totally a word—makes the rum seem ever rummier, therefore making my Dark 'N' Stormy that much more yummy. The only thing that would make it the ducks nuts would be if they used Bundy Rum. I love that shit. Ever since I went to Australia a few years back, it has become my go-to rum. Every time I travel, I buy a bottle or two when I come through duty-free.

The sound of Jesse's voice has me turning my attention to him. "Better luck with the Christmas bake-off." Without stopping, he saunters on by, not giving me a chance to reply.

"*Jackass,*" I growl under my breath and watch his jean-clad ass as he walks away, my anger rising at his flippant remark and his lack of respect. He will NOT win the Christmas bake-off, that prize is mine. I'm going to make what I'm best known for around here at Christmas, rum balls. I have made, and won, the Christmas bake-off with my rum balls for the last three years. And this year will be no different. I'll make the most kick-ass rum balls I have ever made and blow the judges' minds. I will deck my balls like never before. The presentation alone will cause me to win, henceforth kicking his sexy ass to the curb. He's going down, I will not lose to that man again.

Game on, Jesse Thornton, game on.

CHAPTER 10

JESSE

WHEN THEY CALLED MY NAME AS THE WINNER, I was shocked. I was sure Reese and her brownies would win, 'cause those things are the ducks nuts when it comes to brownies. They are chewy, chocolatey, and ohh-so good.

Looking over I see she's got her arms crossed, pushing up her tits. From the scowl on her face, and the quickly diverted eye contact, I get the feeling she's pissed and no doubt my win is the cause of that. It can just add to her hate and animosity toward me. With my win just now, I can't wait for school next week—not!

Passing her on my way to the bar, I offer my condolences on her loss. "Better luck with the Christmas bake-off, Short Stack." I don't stop because the look she gives me, and the anger radiating from her, indicates she's in no mood to chat, and I'm pretty sure she just growled at me too. The sound heads straight to my dick, giving me a semi. Not the time to be sporting a boner, so I think of naked fat grannies and instantly my dick deflates. *Thank fuck for that.*

I head over to the beer tent and order a brewski. While I wait, I lean back against the wooden bar and watch those on the makeshift dance floor. My eyes gravitate toward Reese, she's currently dancing with Drew. The two of them are laughing and cackling, just like always. She looks happy and carefree, I wish she'd be like that around me. Her eyes bright, her cheeks flushed. She's absolutely gorgeous right now, well she's gorgeous all the time but when she's carefree like this, it just adds to her sexiness.

Even though she's blonde-haired and blue-eyed, she's no bimbo. She's one of the smartest people I know, hence why she was valedictorian in senior year. She also happens to be the sexiest blonde-haired and blue-eyed woman I have ever laid eyes upon. She was hot in high school but now that she's pushing thirty, she's a fucking knockout.

Turning back to the bar, I lean against it and pick up my beer. Taking a sip, I choke when someone gropes me on the ass, giving it a squeeze and a pinch. Looking over my shoulder, I'm shocked when I see the pinch came from Reese.

Her eyes lock with mine and when it registers she just squeezed my ass, she groans, "Fuck me," and her face drops.

"Come again?" I say, turning around to face her. Standing up to my full height, I stare down at the pixie before me.

"I'm going to kill her," Reese mumbles to herself.

"Kill who?" I question.

"My ex-best friend."

"Why?" I ask, confused as to why she wants to kill Drew when she just groped my ass.

"She dared me."

"Dared you to what?"

"Pinch the sexy ass of the guy leaning against the bar."

"You think my ass is sexy, Short Stack?" I tease.

"Of course that's the part that you'd pick up on AND stop with the Short Stack."

"It takes a sexy ass to know a sexy ass."

"What does that even mean?"

Shrugging my shoulders, I take a sip of my beer and stare down at her. "Did you get shorter?"

"Fuck you, jackass. I don't tease you for being a giant."

"I'm not a giant, Seven Feet Pete is a giant. I'm six foot two, which is a normal, more acceptable height. Just look around."

"Whatever," she huffs. "It's not nice to tease people about their height, or lack thereof, in my case."

"It's not teasing, even Pete refers to himself as Seven Feet Pete."

"Not the point," she snarls. She grabs my beer from my hand and takes a drink. I watch her lips wrap around the rim of the bottle. Ohh crap, my semi is back. With her eyes locked on mine, she chugs back my beer. Slamming the empty on the bar top beside me. She licks her lips and my eyes follow her tongue as it sweeps across her plump bottom lip. I want to trace her lip with my tongue.

We silently stare at one another—the atmosphere around us pinging—not with hatred but something else, something similar to when we were at the lake that one time. Without thinking, I reach out and brush a blonde lock of hair behind her ear; a spark jolts through me when I touch her. She smacks my hand away. "Rude much?"

"Huh?"

"Touching me without my permission."

"This coming from the woman who just groped my ass."

"Whatever," she snaps. "Just keep your hands to yourself."

She spins around and storms away from me. Her sexy ass swaying from side to side with each step she takes. She joins Drew and Rusty, who are now sitting by the dance floor. She picks up her bag, leans down and hugs Drew, and leaves, storming out of the beer tent.

Turning back to the bar, I pay for the drink Reese drank. I decline another and decide to call it a night myself.

Climbing into my Jeep, the engine turns over and "She Hates Me" by Puddle of Mudd blasts through the speakers. It's kind of appropriate after the run-in I just had with Reese.

Shaking my head, I grin when I think about the feisty little spitfire. She fucking hates me, but I'm going to change her mind. She did once before and I'm sure I can change her mind again. There's something about Reese Turner. My interest regarding her has been there since high school, and now that I'm back, that interest has fired up once again. We have a connection, I know she feels it too but for some reason, she keeps denying the attraction. I can't stop thinking about Reese and what happened when I brushed the hair off her face just now. Something sparked between us and I'm going to make her fall to her knees before me, again.

...Three weeks later

"ARE YOU KIDDING ME?" I GROWL, STEPPING OUT OF my car, I slam the door and turn around. Coming face-to-face with *him*, Jesse Thornton. My arch nemesis. At every turn he's pissing me off and now, his big-ass Jeep just ran into the back of Betty Beetle.

"Yo, jackass, where did you get your license," I shout at him, "from the Wheaties box?"

"Calm your farm, Short Stack," he says, his voice deep, rough, and calm.

"Do not tell me to calm my farm when you just crashed into Betty."

"Who the fuck is Betty?"

"My car, Betty Beetle."

"You name your car?" he questions me.

"Don't you?" I sass back at him.

"Ummm, no," he snaps, "and normal people don't either."

"I do," Drew says from next to me. "Mine is Molly Mini and Rusty's is Rodney Ram."

"You are all certifiably insane."

"At least we can drive," I scoff. "You better have insurance."

He grips the back of his neck and I immediately begin to fear he doesn't. "Of course I do, what kind of idiot do you think I am?"

"A big one."

He rolls his eyes at me. "So mature, Reese," he snaps, just as Sheriff Andy Isack rolls up.

"Fuck," I mumble.

Jesse turns around to face the sheriff, a smirk on his gorgeous face. "Sheriff," he greets Andy, shaking his hand.

"Reese Turner," Sheriff Isack says, a teasing tone to his voice. "What have you done now?"

"What makes you think it was my fault?" Jesse snickers and I glare at him.

"It generally always is," he says, grinning at me.

"Touché," I say, shrugging my shoulders. I'm not the best driver and over the last few months, Betty has been in the repair shop more than she's been at home with me. "But this time, it was him." I point to Jesse. "He ran into Betty."

"And to think, you just had her bumper repaired."

"Again," Jesse says, smirking like the jackass he is. "You should be due for a freebie by now."

"Guess I will be, since YOU will be paying this time,"

I sass back. His face drops at my words. *Suck on that, Jerkface*, I think to myself as I watch him walk over to the tow truck driver who's just pulled up.

The three of them chat and laugh like little old ladies. My eyes are locked on Jesse, he throws his head back and laughs. In the afternoon light, he looks so carefree and like sex on a stick. It's such a shame that a good-looking man like him is a mega asshole.

Rusty arrives just as our cars are towed away. Turns out Jesse's brakes failed, causing him to run into me.

"What'd you do this time?" Rusty asks me, after kissing Drew hello.

"For once it wasn't my fault."

"First time ever," he teases.

Sticking my tongue out at him, I laugh. I know I'm not the best driver but finally, I'm involved in an accident that I didn't cause. "Jesse ran into me and busted Betty's ass."

"Whose ass did I tap?" Jesse asks, joining Rusty, Drew, and me.

"You didn't tap my ass, you busted my ass." As soon as the words leave my mouth, I realize what I said and my eyes widen in embarrassment.

"Holy shit, Reese," Drew says, with a laugh, "that's the funniest thing you've ever said." She's now doubled over, holding her stomach with tears pouring down her face.

Flipping Drew the bird, I shake my head but my mouth lifts in a grin because that really was funny.

Looking back at Jesse, I scowl. "I can't believe you hit Betty," I say, my voice laced with venom.

"And I can't believe you name your car, that's just stupid," Jesse snaps back at me.

"Now, now, Jesse," Rusty says, "no need to be harsh."

"Ohh, that's right, you all name your cars."

"We should name yours," Drew says, with a twinkle in her eye.

"Yes!" I shout with glee and clap, while Jesse growls, "Hell no."

"Just give in, dude," Rusty interjects. "It's the easiest way with these two." He flicks his finger between Drew and me.

"Johnny," Drew shouts. "Yours is Johnny Jeep."

"Yes," I say, "that's perfect." And in my mind I have renamed him *Jerkface Jesse*.

"God help me," Jesse says, just as his mom pulls up.

She rolls down the window, "I hope you apologized to Reese for hitting Betty."

"Really? You know her car's name?"

"Yes, everyone knows about Betty, and for your information, this here is Penny Pontiac." His mom pats her steering wheel, showing Penny the affection that a car deserves.

"Fuck me," he mumbles under his breath.

"Jesse Thornton," she scolds him, "language, I raised you better than that."

"Sorry, Mom," he says. A sheepish look on his face, as he climbs into the passenger seat of his mom's car. He looks out the window and lowers the glass. "Reese, I'll leave my insurance details on your desk in the morning."

"Thank you." I nod and smile.

"And, Short Stack, I'm sorry for hitting Betty." His sincerity warms my heart, and I grin at him saying Betty.

Standing on the sidewalk, I watch them pull away. *I wish he could be like that all the time* I think to myself with a sigh. "What's the sigh for?" Drew questions, throwing her arm around my shoulder.

"I'm without Betty…again," I dejectedly reply, leaning my head on her shoulder.

"Maybe we should get you a bicycle?"

"I'd rather walk, thank you very much." I'm not the most coordinated person in the world. Me and bicycles go together like oil and water, as in, we don't. The last time I tried to ride a bike, I ended up in the hospital with a broken wrist and a concussion. I hit the back of a garbage truck and landed in it; like in the trash compartment back of a garbage truck. I've never been on a bike since, and I never will.

"Ohh yes, the great bike crash of nineteen ninety-eight," she teases.

"Yes, that," I sass back. Looking to Rusty, I smile sweetly. "Rusty, do you think you can drop me home?"

"Of course," he says,

"And maybe stop via the liquor store and supermarket?"

"It'll cost you."

"What's the going rate for these favors?" I ask him.

"A batch of brownies," he hesitantly says.

"Deal."

The three of us climb in Rodney Ram and Rusty chauffeurs me around before dropping me home. As I climb out, I promise that I'll have a batch ready for him in the morning when he picks me up for work. Luckily for him, he also works at Willow Grove Elementary, so it's not out of his way. He and I are both teaching the third grade this year and I have to say, it's been fun working alongside my bestie's husband. He's great with the kids and one of these day, he'll make a great dad too.

After unpacking my groceries, I spend the rest of the evening baking Rusty his brownies and thinking about Jesse, wishing I could stop thinking about how sexy he looked in the afternoon sun earlier. I can't fall for his charms again, he broke my heart once, I cannot open myself to heartbreak like that again.

Mom drops me home and when I walk inside, I head straight to the fridge and grab a beer. I pop the cap and take a sip, sighing as the cool liquid slides down my throat. Flopping down on the couch, I flick on Netflix, lie back, and watch an episode of *Housewives of Beverly Hills*; it's my 'I'll take it to my grave' secret guilty pleasure. The antics those women get up to amaze me, it really is addictive television. It also helps that they're smokin' hot, albeit a little crazy at times...reminding me of a sexy crazy someone in town that I know.

The episode ends and I head into the kitchen. Placing the empty in the recycling, I grab another beer and go into my office. I have a few things to catch up on and my delayed arrival home didn't help. Nor did watching Housewives, but you get that.

Sitting at my desk, I think over the afternoon and groan in frustration because I should have known better.

The brakes had been messing up the last few days but I didn't think it was too serious, guess I thought wrong. Now, I'm up for an insurance deductible and wrath from Reese. Of all people to run into, it had to be her and then the conversation I had with Mom on the way home made it all the more awkward...

...*"All I'm saying is she's a lovely girl."*

"Who hates me," I mumble.

"She doesn't hate you, Jesse. A sweet girl like Reese couldn't hate anything or anyone. But heed my words, Jesse, she's the one."

"Yeah, and how so?"

"Call it mother's instinct. I think this little accident was just what you two needed to push you in the right direction."

"I think it's more likely to get me killed."

"Ohh pishposh, mark my word, by New Year's Eve, you two will be an item."

"I wouldn't bet on that, Mom."

...As Mom's words die off, I start to wonder if Mom's right. Was this accident the push from fate that Reese and I need to finally get together? Or was it the final nail in the coffin? Then I think of how angry Reese was earlier and decide that fate wouldn't be so cruel to do that to me would she? Short Stack sure is a fiery little thing, that's for sure, and I really do believe she'd kill me at the drop of a hat. I feel sorry for the sucker who ends up with her...and sorry, Mom, it won't be me.

Leaning back in my chair, I remember Mom said that I need to apologize with flowers 'cause 'girls love flowers.'

I know Mom's right. I do need to show her how sorry I am, even if it's just to make our work life easier.

Opening my MacBook, I bring up Flowers R Us and order Reese a "Sorry I Hit Your Car" bouquet and me being me, I can't help but make a dig with my gesture when I fill in the card part.

I finish up some work and when I close down, I notice the flyer for the annual Christmas bake-off sitting on my desk. After winning at the county fair a few weeks ago, I feel like entering and it's not just to piss Reese off. Okay, it's ninety-nine percent to piss her off and I really do think I have a chance, BUT Reese does make the best rum balls around and those things deserve to win.

The temptation is too hard to resist so I open my MacBook back up and enter myself, and my snickerdoo-dles, into the Christmas bake-off. It's going to be so much fun competing against Short Stack, and winning; again.

Game on, Reese Turner, game on.

Walking into my classroom, I stop midstep when I see a vase of peonies sitting on my desk, it's a beautiful arrangement in muted purples and pale pinks. With a smile on my face, I walk over and pull the card out.

My eyes pop open when I read the message and a small laugh breaks free.

"I heard that," a deep voice says from behind me.

Spinning around I see Jesse standing in the doorway, he's leaning against the frame, staring at me. He's in dark chinos and a white short-sleeved button-down, his sunglasses hanging from the neck of his shirt. The muscles in his arms bulging from being crossed against his chest. Man, this guy is smokin' hot.

"You heard nothing," I scoff in reply.

"Nope," he says, pushing off the doorframe he enters my classroom and walks over to me. "I definitely heard a laugh, Short Stack."

A growl breaks free at his nickname for me. My eyes betray me and rake over him. The air in my classroom crackles and the temperature rises with each step he takes toward me. He stops before me. Craning my neck, I look up at him and smile. "Thank you for the flowers, Jesse. They're beautiful."

"You're welcome and I really am sorry I busted your car's ass. But I'm mostly glad no one was hurt."

"Just Betty's ass," I add.

He rolls his eyes at me. "Yeah, Betty."

"Well, I'm sorry that Johnny Jeep is in the shop, too."

"My Jeep, will be fine." He places emphasis on the word Jeep and I can't help but grin.

We fall silent; the only sound is the chatter and laugher of the kids out on the playground echoing through the open windows. It's not awkward like it some-time is when it's just the two of us. It reminds me of the night that I let my guard down with him. Shaking away those thoughts, I continue to silently stare at him. The silence becomes deafening but the bell rings, interrupting whatever the hell this was between us just now.

He steps backward, staring at me. "Have a good day, Ms. Turner." Without waiting for a reply, he turns around and begins to exit my classroom.

"You too, Mr. Thornton," I reply, as my eyes watch him and his sexy ass walk away from me.

My students start entering the classroom and all thoughts of Jesse and his sexiness disappear and I focus on my kids.

Throughout the day, my eyes keep drifting to the flowers and I find myself smiling and feeling not so irritated with Jesse. While the kids finish up their art project, I sit down at my desk and my mind, once again, drifts to Jesse. When I put everything into perspective, he really isn't that much of an asshole. Quintin is an asshole. Jesse is just a jackass, a sexy as sin jackass.

From what I've seen since he took over as principal, he really did deserve the position over me. Also I can't be mad about losing at the fair, it's just a baking competition, losing that ribbon wasn't the end of the world. And the accident with Betty and Johnny, was just that, an accident. It's not like he ran up my ass on purpose. No one wants to pay higher insurance rates. Maybe it's time I put it all aside and start being nice to him. What's the worst that could happen?

After all, it's easier to love than it is to hate. Not love-love but like-love, I don't love Jesse Thornton...and I never will.

A SORT OF TRUCE HAS BEEN CALLED BETWEEN REESE and me and over the last week, the dynamic between us has changed. She's not as bitchy as she usually is and dare I say it, she's actually nice to be around. My cell rings. Looking down, I see it's the repair shop. Picking it up, I answer, "Hello, you got Jesse."

"Jesse, it's Darryl at D&K Auto Repairs."

"What can I do for you, Darryl?"

"Just calling to let you know your Jeep is ready."

"That's great, I'll be in to collect it after school. What about Betty?"

"Who's Betty?" he questions.

"Reese's Beetle,"

"Ohh, Betty Beetle," he laughs. "Yeah, it's ready too. I'm about to call her next."

"Don't bother," I tell him, "she's in class now so I'll tell her at recess."

"Okay, thanks."

"See you later today."

The bell for lunch recess rings and I make my way to the teachers' lounge, when I walk in my eyes immediately gravitate toward Reese. She looks really pretty today. She's wearing a pale blue dress with buttons down the front and a white cardigan over the top. Walking over to her, she looks up and smiles at me. It's a genuine smile and it stops me in my tracks. She's hasn't looked at me like that since our 'moment' by the lake in senior year.

"Reese, your car is ready," I tell her as I pull out the seat next to her. She looks over to me and scrunches her eyes in confusion. "Darryl called to say mine was ready and I asked about Betty."

"Dude, you called my car Betty," she teases me, poking me in the arm.

"Whatever," I scoff. "Did you want a lift or not?" My tone is harsher than I intended, causing her smile to deflate. *Dammit, Jesse,* I internally scold myself.

"It's fine," she snaps in reply, putting her bitchy walls up again but with how I snapped, I don't actually blame her right now. "I can get Rusty to drop me off since he's been my chauffeur for the last week."

"It's no trouble. Really." She stares at me. "I'm going there anyway, may as well carpool and give Rusty an afternoon off."

"Well, when you put it like that, a lift would be lovely."

"It's the least I can do."

"You sent me flowers, Jesse, which you didn't need to do."

"It was my pleasure." I smile and she returns it. Her smile lights up her face and I get the sudden urge to lean forward and kiss her. Thankfully, Rusty arrives and the feeling to kiss her dissipates.

"Hey, guys," he says, sitting down across from us. His eyes dart between Reese and me, with a quizzical look on his face. "You two look…cozy," he hesitantly states.

That's when I realize we'd leaned toward one another. Not only was I about to kiss her, but I'd also invaded her personal space. *What the fuck is wrong with me?* More to the point, was she reciprocating my actions? Does she feel this pull too?

We both pull apart, making is obvious to anyone watching that we were in fact in a 'cozy' position together. "I was just telling Reese her car is ready."

"You need a lift after school?" Rusty asks her, biting into his sandwich.

She shakes her head. "Nah, Jesse is going to get Johnny so I'll grab a ride with him."

"You sure?" he questions her, his reaction shocks me.

"Yep, I'm sure." She nods, reiterating her sureness.

She closes the lid on her lunchbox. "I have a few things to catch up on. I'll see you after school, Jesse, and, Rusty, I'll see you tomorrow night at BB's."

Rusty salutes her. "Roger that."

I watch her walk out of the teachers' lounge. My eyes dropping to her ass as she walks away.

"What's going on between you two?" Rusty queries,

snapping my attention back to him and away from Reese and her delectable ass.

"I don't know what you mean?"

He eyes me. "Sure you don't." He pauses, "Blind-freakin'-Freddy can see that the dynamic between you two has changed. For one, it looks like she no longer wants to smother you with a pillow and the biggest change of all, you eye-fucking her just now as she walked away."

"Was not."

"If you weren't, you wouldn't have snapped at me just now." He takes a deep breath and stares intently at me. "I'm going to say this once and once only, don't hurt her again. She's been through enough, she doesn't need anyone else jerking her around."

"What do you mean again?" I ask, not sure what he's getting at. He shrugs as if to say, you know, but I don't. What does he mean by again?

"Exactly that. Just don't hurt her, or I'll hurt you."

"I get that, but why the stern warning? Why you going all big brother on me? What don't I know?"

"It's not my place to say."

"Rusty, you can't warn me off like that and not say anything."

He stares at me, contemplating whether to share or not. It feels like he's not going to tell me anything and then he opens his mouth. "Her last boyfriend cheated on her with his assistant. When it all came out, he took off. She came home after crying on our sofa for two days to an empty apartment. He literally took everything. Leaving her with nothing but Betty, a huge debt, and a broken heart."

"Shit, that's rough."

"Yeah, so don't fuck with her."

Before I can say anything else, he stands up and walks out, leaving me sitting here playing what he said over and over in my mind. No wonder she hates me, well, men. That guy sounds like he's a total jackass, she's better off without him. If she was mine, I'd never hurt her like that. I'd worship the ground she walked on and shower her with love and affection each and every day.

The bell rings, startling me. Looking around, I realize the lounge is empty and I'm alone, some principal I am. Standing up, I make my way back to my office. Taking the long way, so I can walk past Reese's classroom.

As I pass by, she looks up and smiles at me. Our relationship is changing, for the better, and Mom's words about her being 'the one' pop into my mind. I never saw myself settling down but if anyone were to make me change my mind, it would be Reese Turner.

THE REST OF THE DAY FLIES BY AND BEFORE I KNOW it, I'm walking toward administration to meet Jesse so we can head to D&K Auto Repairs and we can pick up our cars. I've missed Betty, I hate being without her and relying on others. You'd think after how many times she's been in the shop, I'd be used to it but I hate putting people out.

Stepping through the door into the admin reception area, I smile when I see Mrs. Thornton is already here.

"Hello, Reese, dear. You look lovely today." She turns to Jesse who's just joined us. "Doesn't she look lovely today?"

"She always looks lovely, Mom," he replies, his words shocking me. My cheeks heat at his kind statement; I wish he could be like this all the time.

"Thank you, Mrs. Thornton, and thanks for the lift. I really appreciate it."

"It's the least I can do since my son hit you."

"It was an accident, Mom," Jesse whines. It's fun seeing him so placid and nice with his mom instead of the jackass he usually is around me.

"He's made up for it, Mrs. Thornton. He sent me a gorgeous apology flower bouquet the day after."

"Ohh, he did, did he now?" She beams at her son's actions.

"You raised a nice boy." *Sometimes*, I silently add.

"That I did." She looks to Jesse and I see nothing but admiration in her eyes for her son. "Well, let's get going. I need to get to bingo early so I can get a good table. I'm not letting that Stefanie woman get the good spot, or win tonight, not after she cheated the other week but today, she doesn't stand a chance. My palm's been itchy all day. That prize is mine."

Jesse rolls his eyes at his mom's superstition, and her rivalry with Stefanie.

He locks up the office and the three of us head toward the exit. Mrs. Thornton leads the way, while Jesse and I follow behind. I giggle to myself as she continues to prattle on and on about Stefanie and her latest antics. The rivalry between the two of them kinda reminds me of Jesse and me. Except ours is real and not over who wins at bingo, or who gets the best seats. Ours is from him being a jackass, breaking my heart, and taking what's mine. Okay, so maybe I'm overreacting a little with the what's mine part but he did break my heart. He was my first heartbreak and that's one you never get over.

It's funny, I'm still heartbroken over what Jesse did to me in senior year but my heart's fine when it comes to

Quintin. Clearly Quintin wasn't the one, not that Jesse is either. He was just the first so that must be it.

Jesse places his hand on my lower back as we walk down the hallway and even though he's not physically touching me, it heats my skin. Closing my eyes, I breathe in deeply, but that's a mistake because I'm assaulted by *him*. He still wears CK One, just like he did back in high school.

We reach Mrs. Thornton's Pontiac in the deserted parking lot. Jesse opens the back door for me. Looking at him, I smile and climb in. Pulling my seat belt on, I'm shocked when the door on the other side opens and Jesse climbs in next to me. Looking over at him, I scrunch my eyes in confusion.

"Mom's front seat is full," he informs me.

He looks like a giant in a small clown car right now, his knees are up around his ears. I hold back my laugh because he looks pissed off and I don't want to be trapped in a car with a pissed-off Jesse, but I can't help myself. I turn to face him. "Comfy?" I snicker toward him, unable to hold back my giggle.

"Very," he sarcastically replies. "It's fine for a short-legged midget like you."

"I think the term you are looking for is vertically challenged."

"Tomato. Tomahto."

"Whatever the case," I add, "my short legs and I are quite comfortable right now. You and your gangly trunks are squished like sardines in a can."

"Bite me, Short Stack," he snaps, staring intently at me.

"You wish, Thornton," I sass back.

He turns his head to look out the window and I'm one-hundred-percent sure I heard him quietly whisper, "Hell yes I want you to bite me."

A short time later, we arrive at D&K. I climb out and then pop my head back in. "Thank you for the lift, Mrs. Thornton."

"You're welcome, dear."

Smiling at her, I stand upright and close the door. She and Jesse chat while I walk into the office.

"Well, well, well, if it isn't my most valued customer," Darryl teases as I walk over to the counter.

"Hardy har har," I heckle. "Maybe next time I'll take it to Guido's instead."

"I love that you know to say next time," he air quotes next time, "and don't be harsh. You're my best customer… ever…and I've been in the repair business for forty-odd years now."

"Hence, why I come here, you are the best…for an old man."

"Respect your elders, missy."

"I'm so sorry, ohh wise old one," I playfully tease.

"Such a smart-ass, when are you going to settle down? Make an honest man out of someone."

"Just haven't found Mr. Right yet." I shrug and sign the paperwork he slides across the counter.

"He may be closer than you think." I notice he's looking over my head, not that it's hard, I turn around and see he's looking at Jesse.

Turning back to Darryl, I shake my head. "Nope, not in a million years, old man. Not in a million years."

"Famous last words." He winks at me and hands me the keys to Betty. "See you soon, Reese," he cheekily adds.

"Bye, Darryl." Turning around, I throw a wave over my shoulder and step out of the office and walk over to Jesse.

"Thanks again for the lift."

"It was my pleasure."

We silently stare at one another, it's awkward but at the same time not. Maybe this car crash was the catalyst we needed to move forward. The honking of a car horn startles me and I jump in fright. This causes Jesse to laugh and with the afternoon light behind him, he looks carefree and hot as hell.

Before I make a fool of myself, I decide to leave. "Have a good weekend, Jesse."

"You too, Short Stack," he says. I ignore the Short Stack comment and walk over to Betty. Her fender is all shiny and pink again; she looks beautiful. "Hey, girl," I say to my car as I unlock the door and climb in. Running my hands over the steering wheel, I smile. "It's good to have you back."

Sliding the key into the ignition, I start her up and drive out of D&K's and head home. Stopping at the liquor store, I pick up a bottle of wine—hey, it's the weekend—and a bottle of rum to make a test batch of rum balls.

Later that night as I climb into bed, I feel happy and slightly tipsy—I may have had a few Dark and Stormies while I was getting my bake on. Everything is right in the world again. Betty is home, the balls I made tonight were the ducks nuts—that ribbon is mine—and Jesse and I are in a good place, finally.

Closing my eyes, I drift off to sleep and dream sexy things about Jesse Thornton and what it would be like to feel the scruff on his face between my thighs.

I'M ON MY WAY TO MEET MOM AND DAD FOR brunch. I'm tired because I didn't get much sleep last night. Every time I closed my eyes, I dreamed about Reese and all the dirty, nasty things I want to do to her delectable body.

Mom smiles when I enter the kitchen.

"Morning, Jesse." She places a kiss on my cheek before she walks over to the coffeepot and pours three coffees.

"Morning, Mom." I kiss her on the cheek and take a seat at the ginormous, island counter in Mom's kitchen. She really has a dream kitchen, hence why she's a super baker.

"You look tired." She passes me a coffee.

"I am. It's been a long week." I pick up the mug, bring it to my nose, and inhale. Taking a sip, the caffeine awakens my senses and gives me a boost of energy.

"Winter break will be here soon."

"Not soon enough," I whine.

Lifting the mug up again, I take another deep breath. I let the smell invade my soul. The scent of coffee is just as cathartic as the liquid itself. Finally, I feel awake and at peace with the world. Closing my eyes, I take another sip and savor the flavor and let the warmth of the brew envelop me.

"Should your mother and I leave you and your coffee alone, Son?" Dad teases, slapping me on the back as he takes a seat next to me.

"Hardy har, old man."

"Ease up on the old."

"If the old shoe fits," I taunt in reply, earning myself a smack up the side of the head.

"You're never too old for a spanking, Son."

Raising my hands in defeat, I joke, "Fair enough…Grandpa."

Dad shakes his head at me but when I glance back over at Mom, I see 'the look' on her face and then I realize what I said. *Ohh shit, here comes the 'when are you going to settle down and give me grandbabies' lecture.*

Three.

Two.

One. "When are you going to make us grandparents?" Mom asks, as she transfers brunch to the serving platters.

"Moooom," I complain, like I always do when the grandbabies conversation comes up. "First I'd need a girlfriend and second, I'd need a girlfriend."

"Reese is single," Mom interjects, handing Dad the cutlery and plates to set the table.

"Reese Turner?" Dad questions.

Mom nods. "Yes, she and Jesse were together yesterday afternoon."

"Mom, we were not together, together. We just happened to be picking our cars up from the same place."

"I heard you had a run-in with her and Betty."

"Not you too," I whine.

"Hey, I don't name mine but I can appreciate those who do." He looks to Mom, and I see the love he has for her etched on his face. They've been together for thirty-six years and I think they love each other just as much today as they did back then. If not more. They have the kind of love that I want, I just haven't found the person to reciprocate that all-consuming love as yet.

"Jesse, Son, don't listen to your mother. You'll know when you've met 'the one.' They will annoy you to no end," he looks over to Mom, "love you, Jen Jen." He turns back to me. "But at the same time, you can't stop thinking about them. They're your first thought when you wake, and your last thought of the evening. They consume you mind, body, and soul."

"Who knew you were such a softie?"

"I did," Mom coos, as she finishes dishing up.

We take our seats at the table, and as I eat my breakfast, I think about Dad's words and surprising me, an image of Reese comes to the forefront of my mind. The two of us are sitting on the front porch steps or our two-story Victorian. Her back to my front, my hands are resting on her swollen belly and we're watching two mini versions of us chase a black Labrador around the front yard. It's so vivid and leaves me feeling all giddy.

After brunch with Mom and Dad, I head to Home Depot to pick up a few things. I bump into Drew and Rusty in the middle of the bathroom accessories aisle. "Hey, guys," I offer in greeting.

"Jesse," Drew curtly says, immediately ignoring me, she looks to Rusty. "I'll be in the bedding section." She turns around and walks, no stomps, away from us.

"She's clearly Team Reese."

Rusty laughs, "I don't know what her problem today is." Then he dejectedly adds, "I think it's that time of the month."

"Dude, I don't want to know that about your wife."

"Well, it means we aren't pregnant."

"Ohh."

"Yeah, ohh. Bring on tonight so she can get drunk and we can forget about it for a few hours."

"I'm sorry to hear that. I didn't realize you were trying."

"We have been since we got married."

"You've been married for a few years now?"

"Yep," he says letting the 'p' pop. "I want to give up trying, let it happen naturally but Drew is determined to become a mom. I think the pressure is adding to why we can't conceive."

"Maybe," I agree, I have no idea about this stuff so I'm really no help. "Well, I hope tonight helps you both."

"She'll chat and drink with Reese, and I'll play desig-nated driver and be the responsible one. They'll drink like they think they're still in college and if I'm lucky, I'll get laid before she passes out."

"Good luck with that."

"You should come."

"I'm not really into the threesome thing," I tease, "plus, you're not really my type."

"Hardy fuckin har," he sniggers, "I meant to drinks."

"Tonight?"

"No, next year. Of course tonight. I could use the company."

"Ohh, so it's a pity invite to keep your miserable ass occupied."

"It's not like that...even though it seems like that."

"I'll think about it."

He heads off to find his wife and I wonder if I should join them tonight. Reese and I are in a good place, but will I be overstepping the mark joining them?

After putting in a load of laundry, I collapse on my sofa. I lean back and close my eyes. Once again, a vision of Reese appears before me. She's wearing that sexy as fuck dress with the buttons down the front, her hair cascades over her shoulders. She's smiling and it lights up her face. With a sigh, I open my eyes. "Shit," I mumble to the empty room. "I've been thinking about her again." Ever since Dad's 'the one' speech earlier this morning, she's been at the forefront of my mind. Hell, I swore I saw her everywhere I went today.

Even the sky is fucking with me today; it's a blue-gray color that reminds me of her eyes.

My phone beeps with a text. Lifting up, I pull it from my pocket.

RUSTY: *You in tonight?*

I read over his text several times. It's like the universe is trying to get Reese and me together. First Mom and her words the other day. Then Dad at brunch this morning, and now an invite from Rusty to drinks tonight with him, Drew, and Reese. I mull it over and think, *why not?* A night out drinking sounds good, maybe I can get drunk with Drew and melt some of her iciness toward me.

JESSE: *Sure, got nothing else locked in*
RUSTY: *Great. We will be at BB's at 7*
JESSE: *See you then*

Throwing my phone onto the sofa next to me, I wonder what tonight will bring.

By the time Drew and Rusty pick me up, I'm well on my way to tipsy, maybe even slightly past tipsy. I woke up in a pissy mood because I slept like shit. And it's all Jesse Thornton's fault; damn sexy jackass that he is. Every time I closed my eyes, he appeared in my mind. He did wicked, wicked things to me and my body.

At around 3:00 a.m. I couldn't take the arousal anymore, I reached into my top drawer, grabbed Buzz, and went to town. A few glorious minutes after I turned Buzz on, I ended up in Orgasmicville. Even after my self-induced orgasm, I was still in a foul mood. Just after sunrise, I climbed out of bed and decided to get some baking done.

Baking always makes me happy, but not today.

Everything I made was a disaster.

My cake stuck to the bottom of the pan. My icing was too sweet and runny and then I burned my snickerdoodles, and that pissed me off more than anything. I kept thinking about Jesse-fucking-Thornton and his winning doodles. It's completely unreasonable to be pissed at him for that, but I don't care, I need to blame someone so I'm choosing him.

After lunch, I decided to try my hand at my rum balls. Well, that was a disaster and a half, mainly because I drank most of the rum. I ended up with plain old chocolate balls, but they were delicious so I finally got a baking win, technically. *Go me.*

I cleaned up the kitchen, made myself a strong coffee to sober myself up a little and then I jumped into the shower to get ready for tonight. Glad for the distraction that a night drinking with Drew and Rusty will bring.

I make a vow to myself to not think of Jesse Thornton.

Just after five, they pick me up and we head over to Bonza Burgers. I was glad we were eating because I needed something to soak up what I've already drunk, the coffee while getting ready did nothing for my tipsiness. I need to be in top form so I can start on round two with my best friend and her husband.

After we all devour a double bacon cheeseburger and wash it down with a homemade ginger beer, we head over to BB's for our night of drinking, dancing, and shenanigans. Drew and I grab a booth, while Rusty heads to the bar.

"I'm so full," Drew says, leaning back, resting her hands on her stomach.

"Me too. Bonza sure knows how to make a mean double bacon cheeseburger."

"I can't believe you eat that crap and stay so thin."

"Says the thin one."

"Wish I wasn't thin," her eyes well with tears, "I wish I was fat and pregnant, sitting here watching you and Rust drink yourselves silly."

"Ohh, babe," I say. Reaching across the table, I squeeze her hand. "It will happen when it's meant to."

"What if it never happens?" she cries.

"Don't think like that. You need to have as many positive thoughts as you can."

"I'm trying, Reese, I really am, but after both of us testing fine, we should be pregnant by now. Why can't I get pregnant?" The tears finally break free, I knew they would come, but I didn't think it'd be this early in the night.

Shuffling out of the booth, I slide in next to her and pull her in for a sideways hug. I let her get it all out, I don't say anything because I know nothing I say right now will ease her pain.

"You really are the bestest friend in the whole entire world, you know that, don't you, Reese?"

"Well, since *I* have the bestest friend in the whole entire world, I don't know how I can hold that title."

"It's one we share equally." She looks up at me and sniffles. "I really am lucky to have you."

"And when you get pregnant, Baby Richards is going to have the most kick-ass parents and aunty in the history of kick-ass parents and aunties."

She smiles, a genuine one, and I know she'll be just fine. She pulls me in for another hug. Wrapping my arms around her, I squeeze her back. I feel her breath hitch and when she pulls back from me wide-eyed, a feeling of unease washes over me. "You may not feel so kick-ass when you see who's at the bar with Rusty."

Looking over my shoulder, I see none other than Jesse Thornton next to Rusty. And then much to my amazement, the two of them turn and head our way, together. Fuck me sideways, he looks hot as hell tonight, but any hotness evaporates when he opens his big, fat, stupid mouth.

"Drew. Short Stack," I offer in greeting. "Drew you look lovely and Reese you look—" My eyes rake over her body; I'm at a loss for words at how gorgeous she looks tonight. But clearly, I've already said something wrong because Reese is currently shooting daggers at me and is ready to explode.

"I'm what?" she snaps. "Grotesque? Fugly?" She stares intently at me, waiting for my reply. I'm confused why she thinks I think that. And right now, if looks could kill, I'd be six feet under.

"No," I say in reply, shaking my head side to side. "I have no words. Reese, you...you look—"

"Just spit it out, Jesse. I'm what?" Her anger takes me by surprise.

"You look beautiful tonight, Reese. Absolutely beautiful." And that's the God's honest truth. She always looks pretty but tonight, fuck me sideways. Her hair is down and she's wearing a dress that hugs her curves and shows off her amazing tits. It's sexy as hell and it would look so much better scrunched in a ball on the floor in my bedroom.

Her eyes widen in shock at what I said. Her mouth opens and closes a few times, she's at a loss for words. I don't think I've ever seen Reese Turner speechless. *Score one for me.* "Well, thank you," she snaps, her tone raised and not at all in sync with her thank you. Then she shocks me when she says, "And you look pretty spiffy tonight too."

Spiffy, I think to myself, I've never been called spiffy before but I'll take it.

Reese and I continue to stare at one another. Neither of us giving an inch. While Reese and I have our silent Mexican standoff, Rusty stands awkwardly next to me and Drew sits next to Reese with a look on her face that I can't read.

Finally, Rusty clears his throat, and Reese looks to him. He nods toward Drew in a 'move, I wanna sit next to my wife' kind of way. Reese shuffles out of the booth, letting Rusty sit next to this wife, and she slides into the booth across from them. In sync, all three of them turn their heads and look up at me, standing here like a fool.

"Well, are you going to sit?" Reese asks me.

Nodding, I sit down on the edge, as far away from Reese as possible, I don't want to be in scratching or drink throwing distance. I can feel her presence beside me, even though I'm balancing precariously on the edge of the booth seat, trying to stay away from her.

The four of us fall into conversation, laughing and

telling stories from high school, college and what each of us have been up to over the years. With each drink we consume, I find myself moving closer and closer to Reese. I'm being pulled toward her by an invisible force.

After a few more rounds, I notice our bodies are now pressed tightly together. She hasn't pulled away and I like feeling her against me. Do I wish we were at home naked? Hell yes I do, but baby steps, that will come later...maybe...I hope.

Every time she moves, I smell the coconut of her shampoo and my eyes drift down the top of her dress—hey, I'm a man—and Short Stack has the nicest fucking tits around. I can't determine if she's wearing a bra or not but whatever the case, I fucking love what this dress does to the girls. I remember the feel of her breasts from high school, they're a little bigger now but they're still plump and gorgeous and I'd love the chance to press my face into them and motorboat her.

Both Drew and Rusty catch me perving on her, multiple times, but each time they raise their eyebrows suggestively at me. It's like they are egging me on to make a move, or I'm just a little drunk and reading into things.

Leaning back, I watch Reese animatedly recount a story about one of the kids her in class who, for show-and-tell, tells a story about LEGO pieces and his cousin's butt and pooping bricks. We all laugh when she's finished and I notice that it's *her* leaning into me this time.

It's like all of a sudden, we're drawn to one another, like moths to a flame...and that's the perfect analogy for us. We burn hot around each other, but it's not in a sexy fun way, it's in a fiery inferno, ready to engulf us at any moment kind of way. It could be the beers and the shots talking, but I don't care if I get burned.

After Reese's story, Rusty drags Drew to the dance floor, leaving us alone. It's silent between us, except for our loud heavy breathing. It's awkward and stilted. "Can you let me out, please?"

"Huh?" I ask, her words not registering, I'm too busy admiring her beauty, and her tits.

"Can you move, please? I need to use the bathroom."

"Ohh, right. Yeah. Sure." I'm babbling but Reese doesn't seem to notice.

Shuffling out of the booth, I watch her as she heads toward the restrooms. A few moments later, she returns and before she sits down, she reaches over to grab the food menu from the caddy. She gives me another glorious view down the top of her dress and from this angle, it confirms to me that she isn't wearing a bra. *Jackpot.*

My eyes drift down her sexy body as she leans over. My gaze lingers on her ass, I have to hold back a groan and stop myself from lifting my hand and massaging the globes of her delectable ass. She stands back up and reads the menu.

"I'm going to order something to eat." She peruses the menu. "You want anything? I'm thinking loaded cheese fries."

Standing up to let her back in, I grunt when she says cheese fries. I'm not in a cheese fries mood, I'd prefer wings and the wings here are great, especially with beer so it's win/win. "Really? All that grease and fat, why—" But I don't get the finish my sentence. She spins around, her face red with anger. She flicks her hand out and it collides with my balls.

For a little thing, she sure has a wicked right hook.

Doubling over, I hold my balls. Lifting my gaze to hers, I growl, "What the fuck is wrong with you? You just decked me in the balls!"

MY EYES WIDEN WHEN I REALIZE THAT DUE TO MY height, or lack thereof, I just hit Jesse in the balls and not his stomach, like I was aiming for. He's doubled over and groaning in agony. I know what it's like when you smash your vag bone, so I presume it's much like getting hit in the balls. I'm about to apologize, when he yells at me. "What the fuck is wrong with you? You just decked me in the balls!"

"It was an accident!" I angrily explode back at the jackass.

"Accidentally on purpose," he sneers and mumbles something else under his breath, but I can't hear it. From the look on his face right now, I know it was something snarky about me.

That's the final straw and I explode, "You, Jesse Thornton, are a fucking dick."

"And you, Short Stack, are a stuck-up sexy bitch."

"Did you just call me a bitch?" Resting my hands on my hips, I glare up at Jesse. It's times like these that I hate being short, staring up at someone when you're angry just doesn't cut it.

"If the shoe fits," he snaps back at me.

"Gah, you are so frustrating." I throw my hands up in anger, he flinches, probably thinking I'm going to deck him in the balls, again.

"Says the frustrating one," he pauses and then with a sneer tacks on, "Short Stack,"

"Stop fucking calling me, Short Stack!" I screech like a banshee. My blood is boiling right now and if I was a violent person, my fist would become acquainted with his face any second now.

"These two just need to fuck already," my soon-to-be ex-best friend mumbles to her husband from behind me.

Jesse and I snap our gazes over to Drew and Rusty, I was so focused on Jesse, I hadn't seen them return. Glaring at my best friend, I snappily say, "Don't make me kill you too." Then I quietly murmur to myself, "Planning one murder is enough."

My comment clearly was louder than I anticipated because Jesse says, "Case in point, you're a bitch. It's a shame your sexy exterior surrounds such a horrible person."

"Says the horrible person. You've been nothing but a jackass to me since...since forever."

"How so?" he says, curiously looking at me. The intensity of his gaze causes my body to quiver, a vast difference to how I feel about him mentally.

"Where do I begin?"

"The beginning is always a good start," he sneers.

Taking a deep breath, I step toward him. *Big mistake.* His cologne hits me and something stirs within, heating my already thrumming skin. My body is buzzing with hatred for the man before me, yet my blood and traitorous vagina, thrum with desire. Lifting my gaze, I look up at him. His intense blue eyes stare back down at me. My eyes drop to his lips. Lips I suddenly want pressed against mine. Against my skin, my breasts, my clit. I want his lips, and tongue, all over my body.

"Well?" he growls, the sound of his voice brings my attention back to the present and away from my dirty thoughts.

"Well what?" I ask, stepping back from him. His closeness becoming too much and unsettling me.

"You were going to explain how I'm an asshole."

"Jackass, not asshole."

"Same, same," he retorts, angering me further.

"Okay, I'll tell you why you're a jackass," I emphasize the word jackass. "You've taunted and teased me since school. You give me the most amazing night of my life and then you tell your friend it's nothing. You hit my car. You took my job. You just called me fat. You won the bake-off—"

"This is over a fucking baking competition?"

"It's more than that," I reply, my eyes welling with tears. Everything I've felt for this man is bubbling to the surface. The anger, the lust, the heartbreak. It's all whirling around becoming overwhelming.

"You really are delusional, Short Stack." He steps toward me, once again invading my space and causing me to lean back to stare up at him. *I hate being short.* I rake my eyes up his chest to his face. Staring into his eyes, I notice his gaze raking over me. His eyes are hooded and eating me up. His reaction is totally confusing right now. "You need—"

"Need what?" I breathlessly interrupt him. His close proximity is doing things to me right now that are the complete opposite of how I feel. I'm feeling sexy things and I shouldn't be wanting them, especially with *him*, not when I'm angry and hurt.

He squats down to my height, leaning into me. His breath hot on my skin causing it to break out in goose-bumps, he whispers, "You need to be fucked good and hard, Short Stack. You need me, no want me, to strip you out of this sexy little dress." He slides his finger down the strap and across my collarbone. "Then you want me to fuck you with my tongue and fingers until you're a wriggling, wanton mess. The most intense orgasm of your life will detonate and you'll be screaming my name for everyone in three counties to hear. Once you've gained composure, you'll push me to my back, straddle me, and sink yourself onto my cock. Gripping your gorgeous tits in your hands. You'll massage them, pulling on your nipples as you ride me until you come again. This time, you'll come harder than when you came on my tongue and fingers."

Swallowing deeply, my cheeks darken at the scenario he just laid out. My panties are saturated. My clit pulsating between my thighs. My body coming alive at his words. My breathing is labored. I stare up at him horny and confused. He's cool and calm, the compete opposite to my aroused and agitated state.

"Cat got your tongue, Short Stack?" he teases. He utters four words and instantly any desire and want I felt for this man evaporates.

"You're a jackass," is all I manage to say, my brain is mush right now. My emotions are all over the place and I'm about to break down but I won't do it in front of him. Shoving him in the chest, I step around him, and race out of the bar.

Stepping outside, the cool night air hits me and I instantly sober up. I walk down the side of the building and lean against the brick wall. I close my eyes and think over the altercation just now. I'm panting and breathing heavily as I try and process what just went down. I'm so confused right now as I think about everything Jesse just said to me. I groan in frustration when I realize he's right, I want everything he said to me just now. *Fucking jackass.*

WATCHING REESE RUN AWAY JUST NOW, I WONDER IF I went too far with the taunting. Did I finally push her over the edge? Squeezing the back of my neck, I let out a frustrated sigh.

Looking up, I'm met with an open-mouthed and stunned Drew and Rusty. "So, I guess you both heard all of that?" I smile sheepishly at them both.

They each nod their head. Going by the fact Drew is speechless right now, I'm betting, she's plotting my demise after speaking to her friend like that and she's right to be angry at me. I feel like shit for the way I just spoke to Reese, I need to apologize before this gets any worse. Turning on my heel, I race out of BB's in search of Reese.

Reese and I need to talk. Once and for all we need to hash out our differences; she's not getting away from me this time. We need to air all our grievances but most of all, I want to find out how she feels because ever since that night at the lake in senior year, this woman has invaded my heart, mind, and soul.

I meant every word just now and I want every dirty thing I said just. I want it all with her. I want what Rusty and Drew have. I want a love like Mom and Dad and I want her to be my forever. *Mom was right, she's the one.*

Stepping outside, I look around the parking lot and find Reese leaning against the building. Her head is back. Her eyes closed. The lone light above her, makes her glow. She looks like an angel, *my* angel. With the vision before me and my words from what I said inside playing on a loop in my mind, my dick is harder than steel right now.

Standing here, like a creeper, I take her in. She really is gorgeous...until she opens her mouth that is, but after tonight that's all going to change. I'm going to get her to admit her feelings for me and I'm going to get the girl. There's something between us, and tonight, we will face it head-on.

Storming over, I grab her around the waist and pull her into me. Before she has a chance to hit me in the balls —again—I spin her around and press her up against the wall, cocooning her body with mine. Visions of her pressed against that tree, my body cocooning her, flit into my mind and I grin.

Staring down at her, I notice her pupils are dilated. Her breathing is ragged. She swallows deeply and stares back up at me.

Lifting my hands, I grip both her cheeks in my palms and lean down. I press my lips to hers. She doesn't move.

She's frozen. I begin to think kissing her just now is a mistake and I'm about to pull away when she throws her arms around my neck. She pulls me into her and she begins to kiss me back. Her tongue pushes into my mouth, slipping and sliding against mine. She tightens her grip on me, deepening our connection and kiss.

This kiss is full of hate. It's filled with passion, heated, and everything in between. It's carnal and perfect in every way. This kiss sums up Reese and me perfectly. I'm transported to senior year at Ryan's party when I first got to kiss her. Kissing her is just as good as I remember, if not better.

She lifts her leg and wraps it around me, grinding herself onto my thigh, she moans into my mouth and the sound vibrates through my body. My cock hardening further.

"Jesse," she murmurs against my lips. "Please," she begs but it's not in a 'take me now way' it's in a 'what the hell, what are you doing' kind of way. She places her palms on my chest and pushes me back, breaking the connection between us. She stares up at me, her chest rapidly rising.

"What the hell was that?" she breathlessly pants.

"A kiss," I nonchalantly say, resting my palms on the wall beside her head. Trapping her between me and the building. She may have stopped this kiss between us, but we will be discussing us.

"I know that, but why?" she snaps, "Why would you kiss me? You think I'm fat. You hate me. You—"

Shaking my head, I press my finger to her lips, interrupting her. "I don't hate you, Reese. Or think you're fat."

Cupping her cheek in my palm, I rub my thumb along the apple of her cheek. "I—"

She shakes her head side to side, and angrily pushes me back, "I...we...I can't do this, Jesse. We just can't." She ducks under my arm and races back into BB's, leaving me standing alone in the parking lot with a rock-hard cock and an aching heart.

Leaning my head against the brick wall, I sigh when a hand squeezes my shoulder. The action startles me. Looking over, I see Rusty. "Don't give up on her, Jesse."

"Are you serious right now? She hates me and thinks I hate her."

"It's not you, per se."

"Then what is it?"

"It's complicated, Jesse, but I do know that you are exactly what she needs. Just maybe tone back on the jack-assness." He pauses, and stares at me. I squirm at the scrutiny in his gaze. "You really like her, don't you?"

Nodding my head, I smile. "Yeah, I do." *I always have, since the beginning of high school. Since we kissed at Ryan Stott's party in senior year. Since I saw her again on my first day at Willows Grove Elementary.*

"Well, go back in there and tell her that."

"What if she decks my balls again?"

"If she's worth another whack to the jewels, then there's your answer."

I laugh and grin back at him. "She is. She really is."

"Good, now get back in there. Win the girl and win me a hundred bucks."

"You and Drew bet on us?"

"Yep. Drew bet that you'd wimp out, leave, and piss

Reese off even more. I said you'll man up and get the girl."

"You have that much faith in me? In us?"

"Yep...I work with the two of you and I have eyes. I see the looks you two give each other when you think no one's looking."

"Pfft, she looks at me with hate."

"No, my friend, she doesn't. She looks at you the way Drew looked at me when we first started dating. With little Cupids floating about, shooting arrows of love around the place."

"She doesn't look at me like that."

"Maybe not right this second, but I assure you, at times, she does...just like you do."

"Bullshit," I scoff in reply.

"Yes, shit. Now go in there and fix this."

"How?" I ask him because I have no clue how to fix this. It's not like a quick fuck will have the magic answer but if that's what I need to do, I'm willing to try. However, I know Reese, she isn't the quick fuck kind of chick. She deserves the world, and I think I'm the man to give her exactly that.

"Ask her to dance and go from there."

"You really think a dance will fix this?"

"If that kiss I just saw is anything to go by, then fuck yes it will."

Nodding my head, I follow Rusty back into BB's. When we walk over to the booth, Drew looks shocked to see me returning but her shock morphs into a megawatt smile when she realizes that I came back.

"God, you make me sick the way you look at your

husband," Reese tells her best friend, unaware I'm standing here.

"I'm not smiling at that," she tells her. Drew leans across the table, grips Reese's chin, and turns her head toward me.

She looks shocked to see me. We silently stare at one another. "Hi," I say, like a doofus.

"Hi," she shyly says back.

Fuck, this is so awkward but I want her so I put on my big boy panties and I ask her, "Would you like to dance?"

"Would you like to dance?"

Five words.

Nineteen letters,

Five syllables and they leave me speechless and shocked. I was expecting something along the lines of "Reese Turner, you are fired" but nooooo, he wants to dance?

With me?

After I ran away from him?

After I decked him in the balls? Clearly the nut pain is making him do weird things; like kissing the life out of me and now asking me to dance. *What the hell?*

After my brush-off/freak-out, I was sure he'd leave but as usual, Jesse Thornton shocks the ever-loving shit out of me. And the shocks keep coming when I reply with one word that has the power to change everything. "Okay."

He smiles and offers me his hand. I stare at it for a few moments and then I place my palm in his. A jolt of electricity zaps between us and just like outside when he kissed me, my body turns to goo. My blood begins to simmer and parts tingle that shouldn't be tingling in public.

He tightens his grip on my hand and we walk toward the dance floor, it's in between songs right now. It's dead silent us as we wait for the next song. "Need You Now" by Lady A begins to play.

Once again shocking me, Jesse spins me around in a circle and then pulls me into him. It's a total swoon worthy moment and I find myself grinning. "I saw that," he quietly whispers.

"You saw nothing," I refute, but my grin widens because this moment is kind of perfect. What the frig is happening right now? Did I enter an alternate universe when I came back inside? Because this, this is everything and more.

Jesse rests one hand on my lower back and holds my other hand between us. My skin heats where his touches me. I wrap my arm around his shoulder, close my eyes, and rest my head on his chest. My body fits against his perfectly, it's as if we were made from the same cookie cutter. Which is funny since I'm five foot nothing and he's a giant six foot whatever, but size aside, we fit…and it feels right.

We sway to the music, and everything around me fades away, it's just us and Lady A. His heart is racing, much like mine is. And as I listen to the beats, I realize it's in sync with mine. This moment is everything.

Opening my eyes, I realize "The Gambler" by Kenny Rogers is now playing and our swaying is no longer in time with the music. Lifting my head, I glance up at Jesse. He's staring down at me. Something passes between us. A force overtakes my body and I lift to my tippy-toes. The same force has overtaken him too because he lowers his head toward me. Our lips press together, meeting for a sweet and sensual kiss.

Breaking the connection, I rest my forehead on his and stare into his eyes. "Thank you for the dance...and the kisses."

"My pleasure, Reese." His voice is soft and it vibrates through me. My skin and body coming alive just from his presence.

We both fall silent. It's not awkward and I don't want this moment to end, that is until Jesse says, "I think I'm gonna head home." I deflate at his words, and then he adds, "Can I escort you home?"

"I came with Drew and Rusty." Turning my head, I look over to the booth we were in and I find it empty. Looking back to Jesse, I shrug. "Guess I do need an escort after all."

"Then allow me." He takes my hand in his and we walk over to the booth. I grab my things and we start walking toward the exit of BB's.

This about-face is confusing but at the same time, I'm content and happy with this transformation in our relationship, or whatever the hell we are falling into, but I do know that I don't want this new dynamic to change. I follow Jesse out of the bar and we wait in line for the courtesy van, a new service offered to help reduce the number of DUIs around town.

The night air is chilly and I shiver, Jesse drapes his arm around my shoulder, pulling me into his side. His warmth envelops me and I find myself liking being in his arms. A smile graces my face.

"I saw that again," he teases, I smack his stomach, his flat, smooth, and toned stomach. I leave my hand there and I lean farther into his embrace. He places a kiss on my temple and again I smile. Another shiver runs through me, but this time my shiver is from arousal and not the frigid cool air. "I love when you smile like that."

Looking up at him, my grin widens. "I like smiling like this."

Our moment is interrupted when the courtesy van pulls up. The people ahead of us climb in, when it gets to Jesse and me there's only one seat left. "I can wait with you for the next one."

"No, it's cold out. You go now."

"Are you sure?"

He nods his head. "Yes, I'm sure."

"Okay," I nod.

Slipping out from under his arm, I walk toward the bus but before I climb in, I turn around, step back to him, lift to my tippy-toes—damn shortness—and kiss his cheek. "Thanks for a lovely night." I climb up into the van and the door automatically closes behind me.

I'm the first one dropped off, and I'm thankful for that because someone had horrendous body odor. As soon as I step out, I take a deep non-smelly breath and head inside.

Changing into my flannel pajamas, I climb into bed, and stare at the ceiling. I think about Jesse and all that eventuated this evening. We went from one extreme to the next and back again. Typical Jesse and Reese BUT we ended the evening not hating one another.

Underneath it all, he's the sweet and caring guy I remember from that night, that version of Jesse is someone I can see myself settling down with. But then there's also the jerkface arrogant ass who used me in high school and teases me relentlessly now. How can they be the same person? And if I give him a chance, will I get hurt again?

I'm so confused right now.

Now that we've crossed this line into whatever this is, I don't know what to do. I lie awake for hours wondering, where we go from here.

LAST NIGHT WAS NOT WHAT I EXPECTED. I WAS hoping to call a truce with Reese, I didn't expect us to explode the way that we did. And I certainly didn't expect to make out with her, but in the moment, all I could think about was pressing my lips to hers. If we hadn't been in public, I would have fucked her.

And now, that's all I can think about.

Short Stack and I have an undeniable bond and I hope after our truce/reconciliation last night, that we can move forward, together, as a real couple. She and I are meant to be and I'm going to do everything in my power to get the girl. Game on, Short Stack, game on.

After tossing and turning for hours, I decide to get up and go for a run. Cranking the tunes on my iPod, I close the front door behind me and put one foot in front of the other. I run for a good hour and a half and by the time I arrive back home I'm sweaty and panting...and I find myself still thinking about Reese. So much for the run clearing my head of her. I'm still thinking about sliding my cock deep inside of her, seeing her cheeks darken with arousal, and hearing her scream my name as she climaxes...just like she did back in high school.

Dammit, now my cock is rock-hard.

Once inside, I grab a glass of water and then head into my room. Stripping off my running gear, I hop into the shower. Closing my eyes, I drop my head back and let the water wash over me.

With a sigh, I open my eyes and pump some body wash into my palm. When I wash my dick, it hardens from my touch. Gripping my shaft in my hand I begin to pump up and down, squeezing my dick tighter and tighter with each jerk. Sooner than I would ever admit, I spray cum all over the shower wall with a grunt, groaning Reese's name as I do. My eyes snap open when I realize I called out her name. I've never called out anyone's name before but I'm not surprised. Since last night, she has invaded my mind and soul.

Turning the water to cold, I step under the spray to cool those rampant sexy thoughts of Reese-fucking-Turner and get my dick back under control. When my cock is soft, and I'm frozen because it took THAT long to calm down, I climb out, dry off, and change into jeans and a black Henley.

Jumping on the sofa, I flick on Netflix and watch *The Real Housewives of Beverly Hills*.

Dozing off, I wake a few hours later with a kink in my neck from the awkward position I fell asleep in. Sitting up, I groan when I stretch out my kinked body. "I'm too old to fall asleep on the sofa," I mumble to myself as I stand up, moaning and groaning as if I'm a ninety-year-old man.

Walking, well shuffling, into the kitchen, I groan when I see I'm out of coffee. "Fuck my life," I whine. "Looks like I'm heading out for coffee."

Grabbing my car keys, I jump into my Jeep and head to the diner for a much-needed coffee and a late lunch. Parking my truck right out front, I climb out and walk in. The diner smell hits me in the face and I moan.

Walking to the counter, I order a coffee and burger to go. Stepping to the side to wait for my order, I bump into someone. "Shit, I'm so sorry." Turning around, a smile graces my face when I see who I've bumped into. "Hi," I say, staring intently at the stunning woman before me. She looks absolutely beautiful today in her black long-sleeved sweater and denim jeans.

Reese hesitantly smiles back at me. "Hi," she shyly offers, brushing a tendril of hair behind her ear.

"Hi," I reply back, internally scolding myself because I already said that.

The air around us crackles as we continue to stare at one another. The moment is interrupted when the waitress yells, "Order for Reese and Jesse."

"That's us," I say, turning back to the counter. I pick up the coffee marked 'Reese' and hand it to her. Our fingers brush when I pass it over and a spark jolts between us, causing both of us to gasp, that was a big one.

"Do you, umm, wanna take a walk down to the jetty?" I ask, still staring at her.

She nods. "Yeah, I'd like that."

Grabbing my coffee and burger off the counter, we silently exit the diner and turn toward the jetty. Neither of us speaks as we walk side by side along the boardwalk. In unison, we walk toward an empty bench just near the jetty and sit down. Both of us stare out at the water lapping at the shore.

"It's so peaceful here," she says, breaking the silence.

"My favorite spot is out at the end of the jetty just at dusk. The way the water shimmers in the afternoon light is gorgeous."

"I've never been down here at dusk. Only at sunrise. Maybe—" She stops and bites her lip, a look washes over her face and I can't decipher what she was going to say.

"Maybe what?" I probe, leaning into her.

"Maybe we can stay and watch it together?"

"I'd like that," I pause, "and maybe we can get dinner afterward?"

She looks to me, nods, and smiles. "I'd very much like that."

"It's a date," I say, holding back the grin trying to break free. *Play it cool, Thornton,* I internally berate myself, but from the look on her face—which I can now read—she too is excited for our date.

We go back to silently drinking our coffees, staring out at the water.

"Can I ask you a question?" I ask, breaking the silence.

She turns her head toward me and nods. "Go for it."

"Why do you hate me?"

My question takes her aback. She begins to shake her head. "I don't hate you, I just, gah."

"Gah, what?"

"You piss me off with your holier than thou persona."

"How so?"

"You've taunted me since the tenth grade. You used me at that party in senior year, you—"

"Used you how?" I rack my brain trying to work out when, and how, I used her at that party. In my memory, we had an amazing time and then she ghosted me.

"At that party before finals, we connected. We were kissing and we did other things, it was perfect. Then I was about to give you a BJ by the lake and that couple interrupted us so we returned to the party. I went to use the bathroom and when I came back, I heard you with Ryan. You said…" She drifts off, as if she's remembering the moment.

"I said what?"

"It doesn't matter what, but you made me feel like a fool. I didn't stick around to face you and have everyone laugh at me for falling for your charm. I left and then come Monday at school, it was as if what we shared meant nothing to you. You went back to teasing me and being an asshat, so I ignored you but you were relentless with the taunting after that party."

A laugh breaks free, I don't mean to, but for a smart chick, she really is clueless when it comes to the opposite sex. "Don't you know what they say about boys who tease girls?"

"What's that?"

"That they like them?"

"You liked me?" she asks, her voice laced with shock.

Nodding my head, I reach over and take her hand in

mine. "Yeah, Reese, I did back then...and I still do now." She's shocked at my response but I want her to know the truth, so I continue. "I know I came across as a player back then but that was all for show, that wasn't the real me. That night at the lake with you, that was the real me and to this day, I still think about our time together."

"But you laughed with Ryan about me."

"I can't remember the exact details but I assure you, I wasn't laughing at you. I really liked you back then, Reese."

"But you were and still are a jackass to me...most of the time."

"Well, you're a bitch to me most of the time, Short Stack."

"Yeah, I'm a bitch 'cause you're a jackass. I treat people how they treat me. You're a big meanie head most of the time," she pauses, "and stop calling me Short Stack."

"A meanie head, really, Short Stack?" She shrugs her shoulders at me. "Well, I apologize for being a meanie head, but I'm not stopping calling you Short Stack. When I say it, it's an affectionate term."

The air around us begins to sizzle, just like it did last night. It seems once again, our relationship is about to take a happy turn.

"Really?"

"Yes, really, and I'm sorry for everything I've ever done to piss you off."

She grins and it warms my heart seeing her like this. "And I'm sorry for being a bitch."

"But you're my bitch, Short Stack." My eyes widen

when I realize what I just said. "I don't mean you're mine, I just—"

She reaches over and presses her finger to my lips. "Stop, I know what you meant, Jesse. I'm your Short Stack bitch and you're my jackass…jackass."

We both laugh and I love that she feels like she's mine. We sit here looking at the lake and we fall into easy conversation, our hands clasped tightly together as she tells me all about life here since she returned from college, and what her douchehole ex did to her. I tell her about my travels and studying in California.

Time flies by and before we know it, the sun is starting to set. "We better head down the jetty if we're going to see the sunset."

She nods. "Okay, let's go."

We stand up and walk down the jetty. My heart is racing with nerves. The afternoon with Reese has been amazing, unexpected but amazing. I think we've turned a corner in our friendship, or whatever the hell we are now.

Reaching the end of the jetty, I turn around and lean against the railing. Reese does the same and we both stare up at the sky. Tonight's sunset is on point. The sky is a mixture of colors going from red to orange and into a warm mixture of purples and indigo.

"Wow," she says. "It's beautiful."

"It sure is." But my eyes are locked on her.

She looks over at me.

We stare at one another.

Something takes over my body and I step toward her just as she steps to me. Gripping her cheeks in my palms,

I lean down and press my lips to hers. She places her hands on top of mine and deepens the kiss.

As the sun dips below the horizon and the sky turns dark, Reese and I continue to kiss, confirming this really is the turning point for us but like everything else, it's a sharp and stilted turn.

THE NEXT MORNING THERE'S A REALLY LOUD banging coming from my front door, the sound ricocheting through my head. "UGH!" I moan and that three letter word sounds like jackhammers hammering in my brain. *What the hell happened last night?* I think as I try and open my eyes. I squint at the brightness and roll to my side, my stomach lurches from the movement and I feel like I'm going to throw up. "Why did I drink so much last night?" I whisper, as the knocking—aka really fucking loud banging—continues and somehow gets louder.

"Coming," I shout, wincing at the shrillness of my voice slicing through my brain.

Staggering from the couch, where I clearly passed out last night, I walk over to the front entrance and swing open the door. "Jesse," I say with shock at seeing him standing at my door. "What are you doing here?" My head throbs as I stare at the man before me; he's the last person I expected to see on the other side when I swung it open.

"You invited me over last night?"

My eyes bug wide open, "Whaat? I did? When did I do that?"

"When you drunk dialed me at about 2:00 a.m." He smiles and brushes a tendril of matted blonde hair behind my ear. He cups my cheek and stares at me. His gaze heats my skin, bringing my hungover body alive. "You're cute when you're drunk...and very truthful."

My mind is blank right now, I have no recollection of calling Jesse last night...or of anything I might have said to him. "Ohh God, what did I say?"

"How about you let me in? You can eat this," he lifts a greasy brown paper bag from the diner up, "and I can catch you up on the events of last night."

He doesn't seem angry so I guess I didn't make too much of a fool of myself. "Okay, yep. Sure. Sounds good." I step aside and allow him in. The smell of the food causes my stomach to roll and this time, I AM going to vomit. "Shit," I mutter, covering my mouth.

Pushing Jesse out of the way, I race down the hallway, through my bedroom, and into the bathroom. I drop to my knees and empty my stomach into the toilet, I only just make it.

Resting my arms on the seat rim, I continue to vomit and purge my stomach contents and I'm pretty sure the lining of my stomach too. FYI regurgitated rum balls do not taste great.

Suddenly, there's a cool washcloth on the back of my neck. I rear up in shock and the back of my head collides with Jesse's balls. "Fuuuuck," he groans, doubling over and clenching his nuts in his hands. His face distorted in pain. "I was hoping after high school the ball decking would have stopped but clearly, I was wrong." He groans through clenched teeth but there's also a teeny tiny grin on his face too.

"Shitballs," I say, "I'm so sorry."

Without thinking, I push his hand aside and gently begin to rub his balls better. When my brain finally catches up with what I'm doing, my eyes widen and I quickly pull my hand back. "What the fuck is wrong with me?" I mumble, lowering my head in embarrassment.

"There's nothing wrong with you, Reese, and feel free to keep rubbing the boys better, they, and I, really don't mind at all."

Shaking my head, I flick my hand to hit him in the leg at the crassness of his statement but me and my shitty aim, we hit him in the nuts, again. "Fuuuuuuuuuck," he groans through clenched teeth, once again bending over and cupping his junk.

"Shit, Jesse, I'm so sorry."

"It's fine." He waves off my concern. "This is the most action the boys have gotten in a while. I just wish you weren't so rough with them." He pauses and then cheekily adds, "I never picked you as a rough lover, Short Stack."

"Oh my God," I say, burrowing my face in his crotch in embarrassment. Then I realize where my head is resting and I quickly pull back, falling to my ass beside the toilet. "Oh My God, I'm so sorry I just did that. First I deck your balls…twice…then I try to rub them better and then I rub my face on them. What the hell is wrong with me?"

Jesse laughs. "What?" I snap in anger.

"You're still cute when you waffle."

"I don't waffle," I defensively reply, glaring up at him.

"Yeah, ya do. Now, I'm going to find some ice for the boys. You freshen up and then you can join me in the living room."

Nodding my head, I stare up at Jesse from my spot on the floor. He smiles, and fuck me sideways, it's the most beautiful thing hungover me has ever seen. The slight lip lift causes my body to come alive and makes me want to mount him right here. Right now.

He leaves me to grab an ice pack for his nuts and finally, I stand up. Wobbling on my feet, I reach out and grab the counter to steady myself. Looking at my reflection, I flinch. "Ugh, I look like a sea hag."

Quickly, I brush my teeth and freshen up, well as much as I can without a full day of pampering myself. Giving myself a once over, I still look like death warmed up but it's the best I can manage for now. *I'm never drinking rum again.*

Now that I look semi-decent, I walk into the kitchen and find Jesse tidying up the mess I left. "What the hell happened last night?" I voice, walking into the kitchen and looking around at the mess before me. "It looks like a baking bomb exploded in here."

Jesse turns to face me and holds up an empty rum bottle. "Seems the chef got into the ingredients while baking."

Looking around the kitchen, I shake my head and

when my eyes land on the empty bowl on the floor, the events that led to all of this, slowly come back to me…

…Jesse and I kiss as the sun sets. It's beautiful. It's romantic. It's just like a scene from the romance novels I read. He breaks the connection, pulls back and steps back. He stares down at me. His expression unreadable right now. "Reese, I didn't mean for that to happen."

My heart plummets at his words. I should have known he'd be a jackass. "Right. Gotcha," I snarl through clenched teeth, anger building at myself for once again falling for him and his dumb stupid words. I start walking backward, internally scolding myself for falling for the jackass's words and letting them have such an effect on me.

Shaking my head, I spin around and race away from him. Tears welling in my eyes with each step I take back along the jetty. My heart is hurting from being used, again, by him.

Jumping into Betty, I drive home with tears pouring down my cheeks. Opening my front door, I step inside and throw myself down on the sofa and cry. When I'm upset, I bake, so I decide that's what I'm going to do. Standing up, I walk into the kitchen, slip my apron over my head, and tie it up. Once it's tied, I get out everything for my rum balls and I get to it.

My head's a mess and I keep dropping everything. There's coconut and cocoa powder all over the counter. Rum is spilled all over the counter and melted chocolate drips onto the tray. Picking up the bottle of rum, I measure out two more tablespoons and this time I get it into the bowl. Then bring the bottle to my mouth and swig. I shudder at the sharpness of the liquor but I don't care. I finish stirring the mixture and then pop it in the fridge to set a little before I start rolling the balls.

Setting a timer on my phone, I pick up the rum bottle and bring it to my lips again. Turning around, I slide down the wall and continue to drink.

When the timer goes off, I crawl over to the fridge and grab the bowl out. Sitting on the floor, I continue to drink and eat the rum ball mixture with my fingers. Before I know it, I'm two sheets to the wind drunk. I keep thinking about Jesse and how much of a jackass he was earlier.

Grabbing my phone out of my pocket, I dial his number. "Hello?" *he sleepily answers.*

"You'red a jackdass," *I drunkenly slur.*

"Reese?"

"Yepd, it'd meeed."

"Is everything all right?"

"Just'd peachdy, jackdass."

"What?"

"You'red a jackdass."

"I know, I'm your jackass, and you're my Short Stack."

"No, you'red bigd bigd jackdass."

"Are you drunk?"

"A smidgicall," *I giggle, I lift my hand and separate my thumb and forefinger a little, not that he can see down the phone.*

"Alotical I would say."

"It'sd you'red fault."

"How is it my fault?"

"'*Cause you'red a sexy jackdass who confussdes me an youd knowd what? It'sd a secdret.*"

"*What's your secret, Drunky McDrunkerson?*"

"*My wee lil crushd on you from highd school isd stilld derr but youd lookeded throud me as if I wasdent thered. Asd ifd I'md nodoned*"

"*I've always noticed you, Reese. A blind man would.*"

My eyes widen at his words, if he feels like this, why did he regret kissing me earlier? "*You'red a sweet jackdass sometimesd. I wanna do dirty dhings wid youd.*"

"*What dirty things?*"

"*I want to kiss youd like we did earlier, and then I want youd to spankd me before ducking me.*"

"*You really are drunk, aren't you?*"

"*Yepd…why don't youd comed dover and I showd you?*""

"*What?*"

"*Comed over and I canned yelled youd and kissd you and duck youd.*"

"*I canned yelled youd?*" He repeats and it sounds funny but my rum filled brain, can't figure out why.

"*Yeppers…and bringd mored rum, Id nearly out.*" I take another sip, the bottle clanking on the tiles when I place it down next to me.

"*I don't think you need more rum.*"

"*Youd don't know what'd I needded.*"

"*I know you're drunk as a skunk right now.*"

"*Amd not.*"

"*Case in point. Why don't you sleep it off and I'll see you in the morning?*"

"*Me'd like that sexy jacdkass.*"

"Goodnight, Short Stack."

..."Oh my God," I say, as it all comes crashing back to me. My eyes widen like saucers and my cheeks darken in embarrassment. I cover my face and shake my head side to side. "Jesse, I'm so sorry I did that."

"It's okay, but why were you so angry with me?"

I stare at him for a few moments, he looks really vulnerable right now and I decide to go with honesty. Taking a deep breath, I lay it all out. "You kissed me and then immediately apologized for it happening. I thought...I don't know what I thought, but it hurt when you pushed me away." My confession shocks me. I didn't realize how much I actually liked him until he pushed me away. "It's like each time we kiss, you regret it so you push me away."

"I don't regret kissing you, Reese. Not now. Not back then. Never."

"But why did you apologize? Why didn't you run after me? Yell for me to stop, you just let me go."

"I don't know. It wasn't my plan to kiss you but the moment was perfect, so I went for it." He pauses and runs his fingers through his hair in frustration. "I was worried you didn't want it so I apologized."

"Jesse," I say, stepping over to him to cup his cheek in my palm. "That was single-handedly the best kiss of my life. It was a kiss out of the books I read."

"Really?" he asks, his voice laced with shock at my revelation.

Nodding my head, I smile. "Yes, really."

"I really want to kiss you right now...and maybe do some of the things you offered last night too."

"Oh my God," I cry, leaning my head against his chest. He wraps his arms around me and I feel safe and content in his embrace. "I'm never going to live that down, am I?"

"Probably not," he teases. His voice laced with jest.

"Jackass."

"We've established that I'm your Jackass." He places his finger under my chin and lifts my head so I'm staring up at him. "Now, please kiss me, Reese."

"I want that so much, Jesse, but I still taste vomit and I don't want to ruin this…us…again."

"You couldn't ruin it if you tried, Reese."

"You're too sweet, Jesse Thornton."

"I know," he nonchalantly replies with a shrug of his shoulders, I slap his chest and laugh. "But you know what?"

"What?"

"So are you, my sexy sweet, amazing Short Stack." That's the first time he's called me Short Stack and it hasn't pissed me off.

"I don't feel very sexy right now. I feel like death warmed up." Wrapping my arms around his waist, I rest my head on his chest and I feel with everything that I have that he and I will be fine.

"How about I run you a bath and while you chillax, I'll reheat the greasy food I brought to soak up the last of the rum, and we can figure out where to go from here?"

Nodding against his chest, "I'd very much like that."

Lifting my head up, we stare at one another and a feeling of calm washes over me. Finally, after way too long, everything is grand between us.

AFTER LEAVING REESE IN HER BATHROOM, I HEAD into her kitchen but before I get on to reheating the food, I clean up the mess. She's quite a messy cook, but it could also be due to the fact that she was drunk, no plastered, last night.

Pulling out my phone, I bring up Spotify and smile when "Wake Me Up Before You Go-Go" by WHAM! comes on.

Placing what I can into the dishwasher, I fill the sink and start scrubbing the pots and bowls that won't fit in the machine. I've just wiped down the counter and cupboards when I feel a presence behind me. Looking over my shoulder, I see Reese standing there in a satin robe, her hair is on top of her head in a messy bun, and even though she has no makeup on and is majorly hungover, she looks stunning and I'm hoping that she's naked under her robe. "You are gorgeous, Reese."

"You need your eyes tested."

"Nope, twenty-twenty vision here."

"I think you need a second opinion." She glances around the kitchen and her eyes widen when she registers what I've done. "You didn't have to clean up."

"Well, in order for us to eat, I needed to. You're quite the messy cook."

"Can I blame the rum?" she shyly asks with a shrug of her shoulders that causes the top of her robe to slide off her shoulder. I'm hoping it slides all the way down and that she's naked underneath—hey, I'm a man, give me a break.

"I like you when you've had rum. You're quite truthful."

"Can we maybe forget last night?"

"No fucking way," I tease, "I'm hoping what you offered comes true."

"Remind me again what I offered?" she asks, jumping up onto the counter next to me. Her robe falls to the side, exposing her sexy as fuck legs. My eyes drop down and I take her in. *Fuck me, she's gorgeous.* If I thought her shoulder was sexy, fuck me sideways when it comes to her legs.

Lifting my gaze from her legs to her face, I see her staring at me. "So what exactly did I say last night?" she asks, biting on her bottom lip. "I have a vague idea but I want you to confirm, or hopefully deny what I think I said."

"I'll tell you if you drop the robe."

She stares at me and then nods. Lifting her hands she undoes the tie at her waist, my eyes intently follow her movements. When the knot is undone, she spins the tie in her hand and giggles. Dropping the sash, she slides her hands up her sides and grabs the material at her breasts and slowly spreads it open. All I see is creamy skin and then more satin. She slides the robe down her shoulders, dropping it to the countertop behind her. Leaving her in a sexy black silk cami and matching panties.

My cock twitches as my eyes roam over her. My face breaks out into a grin as I take her in. "Fuck me, Reese, you are a vision."

Her cheeks darken at my words. She rests her palms on the counter behind her and leans back. I swallow thickly. "Short Stack, what do you want right now?"

"I want your lips on me."

"Where?" I ask, stepping toward her but stopping before I do something silly like throw her over my shoulder and lower her to the floor where I fuck her. Or I drop to my knees and feast on her.

"Everywhere," she breathlessly says, her eyes locked on mine as she traces along the edge of the silky material covering her breasts.

Closing the distance between us, I come to a stop between her legs. I lean down and kiss across the top of her breasts, nudging her hand out of the way. "Yes," she moans, running her fingers through my hair and gently tugging as I kiss and nibble up her neck toward her ear. Her head drops back and I take her earlobe into my mouth, gently biting on the lobe. She slides her hand down the back of my head, running her fingers through the hair at the base of my neck.

"Kiss me, Jesse," she purrs.

Kissing along her jawline to her chin, I make my way up to her lips. Pulling back, I hover ever so closely to her lips and stare into her eyes. Time stands still as we admire one another, her tongue darts out to wet her bottom lip and touches mine. It sparks something inside of me and I slam my lips to hers. Her tongue presses against my lips and I open, she slips it into my mouth. Our tongues dance and caress one another.

She sits up and wraps her arms around my neck, pressing her chest into me. I slide mine around her waist and pull her closer.

"Fuck me, Jesse," she murmurs against my lips.

"Here?"

"Bed."

Sliding my hands down to her ass, I slip them under her and lift. She wraps her legs around my waist. Turning around, I make my way down the hallway to her room. Placing her on her feet at the end of the bed, we stand here and make out like teenagers at the drive-in on a Saturday night. She slides her hands down my chest and lifts my shirt over my head. Then rakes her nails down my chest. Dropping to her knees, she makes quick work of removing my jeans and briefs in one swift movement, leaving me naked before her.

She licks her lip and bites it. "I fucking love it when you bite your lip like that."

"What, this?" she says and she does it again.

"Yes, that," I say, my eyes locked on hers.

She lifts her hands and cradles my balls in her palm. "I think I owe these guys an apology."

"Apologize away."

She drops her gaze to the boys and she continues to fondle my balls. Gently rubbing them to say sorry for decking them, I fucking love her apology. From down on her knees, she looks up at me and I have a déjà vu moment of that night in high school but this time, we aren't interrupted. This time, she opens her mouth and sucks my balls into her mouth. "Fuuuuck," I groan, running my fingers through her hair.

Closing my eyes, I give myself over to the sensation of her sucking them. I've never had my balls sucked before and I can easily say, it's the best sensation ever. That is until she licks up my shaft, circles her tongue over the tip, dipping it into the slit before she takes me into her mouth. She slides her lips around my shaft, sucking on it while massaging my balls.

This is the best 'sorry for hitting you in the nuts' blow job in the history of 'I'm sorry for hitting you in the nuts' blow jobs.

Reese puckers her cheeks and takes me all the way to the back of her throat. "I'm coming," I groan and I erupt like a geyser. I don't think I've ever come that hard from a BJ. She swallows every last drop. My cock pops out of her mouth and she wipes at the corner of her lips. Standing up, she stares at me, resting her hands on my hips and winks. *Little minx.*

"My turn," I growl.

Gripping her shoulders, I push her back onto the bed. She bounces a few times and giggles. I grab her ankles and pull her to the edge of the mattress. She squeals, not expecting me to drag her and the sound has my cock twitching to life again.

Dropping to my knees, I lift her ankle and lick up her leg, stopping at the junction of her thighs. "You smell like heaven." With my eyes locked on hers, I lower my head and lick her though the satin of her panties.

"Are you overly attached to these?" She shakes her head. "Good." Grabbing the material in my fingers, I tear her panties off her body, baring her to me. Licking my lips, I lower my head back down and lick her from taint to clit.

"Shit," she mewls, grabbing my head, pushing me farther into her. Clearly she likes what I'm doing so I continue to lick and devour her. Never has anything tasted sweeter than Reese-fucking-Turner's pussy. I slip a finger in and she clenches down on my digit, moaning as I slide it in and out of her. Slipping in another finger, her moans increase. Her body writhing in pleasure beneath me. "I'm…I'm coming," she shouts, as her orgasm rips through her. Her body stiffens as I continue to pump my fingers in and out, milking everything I can from her.

When her body goes limp, I withdraw my fingers. Bringing them to my lips, I suck her juices and moan. She lifts her head and stares at me. I beckon her toward me with my finger. She shakes her head and motions me to come to her. Crawling up her body, I cocoon her underneath me and stare down at her. "You look even more gorgeous after you've come."

"You say the sweetest things. Now kiss me, Jesse."

"Yes, ma'am."

Lowering my head, I press my lips to hers. She slides her hands into my hair and scratches her nails over my scalp. I moan into the kiss and my cock is once again rock-hard, pressing into her thigh. She circles her hips, hinting at wanting more. Breaking the kiss, I whisper, "Condom?"

She shimmies up the bed and reaches into her top drawer, where she pulls out a foil packet and hands it to me. Sitting up, I sheath my dick and line it up at her entrance. Staring down at her, I slide inside, her walls hugging my cock snugly. Pistoning my hips, I slip in and out of her. Lifting her leg over my shoulder, I thrust in deeper. Reese lifts her hands and slides them under her cami, massaging her tits. "Take it off," I growl as I pick up my pace. She removes her top, her breasts spilling free. They're gorgeous, just like the rest of her and I can't wait to become acquainted with them.

Dropping her leg, I lower myself down and take a nipple into my mouth, gently nipping and sucking the tip. "Jesse," she moans, as I continue to suck her tit and slide my dick in and out. I'm close to coming again but being a gentleman, I refuse to come until she has. I pinch her nipple and she screams my name as she orgasms. She clenches down on me and I come too. I explode into the condom, my body shuddering at the force behind my climax.

Sex with Reese is so much better than I ever could have imagined.

Collapsing to the mattress beside her, I pull her into my side and kiss her temple. We lie here in each other's arms, panting. Reese snuggles into my side and gently runs her fingertip back and forth on my chest.

She shimmies back and rests her head in her palm and stares at me. "I thought you were making me lunch?"

"I thought we just ate each other?"

Her cheeks darken in embarrassment at my words. "I meant food."

"Well, I guess I better feed, my Short Stack."

"How about we reheat it together, Jackass?"

"I'd like that."

...three weeks later

LIFE WITH JESSE HAS BEEN AMAZING, TURNS OUT THE guy from the lake IS the real Jesse and he was only teasing because he DID in fact like me. Who ever said that boys tease girls they like need to be shot because it's a stupid saying. Honesty is the best policy and if he'd just told me he liked me, we could have been happier much sooner.

Time is flying by but I'm happier than I've ever been. Once we cleared the air about the mishap at that party and all the other shit in-between, we've found our groove and are now living life to the fullest together. As a couple.

Jesse and I spend most evenings together and it ends with us making love before falling asleep wrapped in each other's arms. I've never been a snuggler before but I just love doing it with Jesse. Whether it be in bed, or on the sofa while we watch *Housewives of Beverly Hills* together. The day I caught him home alone watching that was the best day of my life. I can still remember the 'deer in the headlights' look he had when I walked in. I was expecting porn but no, it was the complete opposite of that.

Nothing will match that first day we got together. We haven't had as much sex in one day as we did that day, but my vagina is okay with that. After the greasy lunch Jesse bought over, we spent the rest of the afternoon and evening naked in bed. Ravishing each other and getting to know each other's bodies veeery well. When we ran out of condoms we went with the 'pull out' method.

To this day, I still maintain that he broke my vagina with how much sex we had. I was surprised I wasn't waddling at school the next day, but wasn't going to complain. That day will forever be etched in my mind, and flick bank. Sex with Jesse is off the charts hot and it was totally worth the wait.

He and I are in a happy place, still in the honeymoon phase, but it's natural and I love spending time with him, in and out of the bedroom.

He's my Jackass and I'm his Short Stack.

I actually don't mind him calling me that now because I know it's laced with affection and not malice. It seems he did tease me because he liked me, not because he was a jackass—oops, my bad.

Tomorrow is the beginning of the Christmas fair and the judging of the Christmas baking competition.

Tonight I'm meeting Drew for dinner and drinks at BB's for our bi-weekly catchup, and then I'll head home for an evening of baking. I've banned Jesse from my house tonight, I don't need him sabotaging me and my 'winning' rum balls—I also promised that I would not drink the ingredients this time. To be honest, the thought of rum still makes my stomach roll. But that's a good thing because I'm determined to win this. I refuse to let Jesse Thornton and his snickerdoodles take the crown from me this time. It's game on and you're going down, Thornton.

After school, I head home and get everything out for baking later. I change into my jeans and a slouchy sweater, my jeans are a little tight and I groan when I finally get them done up. I just need the denim to stretch and then I'll be fine. The temperature has dropped drastically in the last few days, looks like winter has arrived but I don't mind 'cause I can rock my boots, scarves, and hats.

Walking into BB's, I spot Drew in a booth and head over to her. "You're glowing," I tell her as I climb into the booth across from her. A smile graces my face when I notice that my uber awesome bestie has a glass of white wine waiting for me. "You are a godsend," I praise her, picking up my glass, I take a sip. Closing my eyes, the crisp flavor hits my taste buds, causing me to moan.

"Would you like me to leave you alone with your wine?" My best friend teases.

"Hardy har har, Drew."

She picks up her glass and I notice she isn't drinking wine. "No wine tonight? Let me guess, vodka, lime, and soda."

"That's correct…but sans vodka."

"Are you sick?" She shakes her head. I stare at her quizzically and then it hits me. My eyes widen in excitement. "Oh my God," I squeal, "are you?"

The smile of all smiles appears on her face as she nods her head rapidly. "Yep, Rusty and I are pregnant." I squeal in excitement, garnering the attention of those also here but I don't care, my bestie is finally knocked up. Climbing from my side of the booth, I scooch in next to her. Wrapping my arms around my best friend, I hug the ever-loving shit out of her in the best congratulatory hug.

"I'm sooooo happy for you guys," I excitedly say. "If anyone deserves to be parents, it's you two."

Her eyes well with tears. "Reese, I'm so scared, yet too freakin' happy at the same time. I'm emotional and cry at everything. Hell, I cried watching the news the other night when they rescued that donkey from the storm drain."

A laugh escapes me and she hits me in the arm. "Ouch," I cry out.

"Don't anger a pregnant lady."

"Are you seriously playing the pregnant lady card right now?"

"Yep, and I will do so until I give birth."

Leaning across the table, I grab my wine and take another sip. "I can't believe you and Rusty are gonna to be parents."

"I know, he's freaking out too. It's really cute though and I just know, he's going to be the best dad." She starts to tear up at the thought of her husband and their child together. "Fucking hormones," she cries and I realize, I too am teary.

"I don't think pregnant ladies are meant to swear."

"Fuck that. I'll swear if I want to, but I promise not to once Peabody comes."

"Peabody?" I question.

"Saying 'it' felt impersonal so we named it Peabody."

"Fair enough." I reach over and squeeze her hand. "I'm," my eyes well with tears again, "I'm just—"

"Emotional and pregnant like me?"

"Very funny," I sass in reply but her words halt me in my tracks. I can't remember the last time I got my period. Shit, am I pregnant too?

Drew and I chat and she eats her weight in chicken wings. I'm so lost in my head over the fact that I might be pregnant, I miss everything we chat about. Drew and I say our goodbyes and agree to meet up tomorrow at the Christmas fair before the bake fair announcements.

After leaving BB's, I stop via the pharmacy and pick up a pregnancy test. I head home and throw everything on the dining table. Not wanting to deal with that right now, I head into the kitchen and start to do what I do best, bake. I'm not ready to start on my balls, so I push the ingredients that I got out earlier aside and I whip up some chocolate brownies. Once they're done, I start on my rum balls.

I lose myself to baking and before I know it, my balls are done. And if I do say so, these are the best rum balls I've ever made. Since I'm procrastibaking: procrastinating by baking, I decorate them four different ways; coconut, chocolate sprinkles, crushed hazelnuts that are soaked in rum, and chocolate coated with holly or little red bows, all handmade from fondant.

It's 3:00 a.m. by the time I'm finished procrastibaking. Once the kitchen is sparkly clean, I turn around and eye the brown paper bag on the dining table. That brown bag has been taunting me for the last seven hours, waving its brown sparkly jazz hands singing "pee on me and then you'll know" all night long.

Taking a deep breath, I growl at the bag, "Fine." Grabbing the offending bag off the table, I walk into my bathroom and take a seat on the edge of the tub.

Opening the box I read the instructions from start to finish, once again, taking my time. I'm procrastareading now. "Suck it up, Bitch," I berate myself.

Standing up, I pull my pants down and sit on the toilet…but I can't pee. Leaning over, I turn the tap on and a few minutes later, I finally pee. My nerves are shot and I somehow manage to NOT pee on the stick, instead getting urine all over my hand.

Fuck my life.

Washing my hands, I kick off my pants, remove my shirt and bra and grab my nightie. I slip it on, the silky material scratching my nipples as it slides down my body. Sliding into my slippers, I head into the kitchen for some water, time to refill my bladder. Grabbing a glass, I fill it up and down three glasses in quick succession.

Walking back into my room, I sit on the edge of my bed and stare at the floor. My mind is all over the place right now and I can't concentrate on anything that I think about. Finally, the urge to pee hits so I head back into the bathroom and this time, I manage to pee on the stick—*Go me.* And not get any on my hands this time either—*Go me again.*

Placing it on the vanity, I pull up my panties and before I wash my hands, I glance down at the stick and immediately I see two pink lines waving their sparkly pregnant jazz hands at me. "Shit, I'm pregnant."

IT'S ALMOST TIME TO HEAD TO THE CHRISTMAS FAIR and I haven't heard from Reese all day, which since we hooked up, is very unusual. I decide to call her but it goes to voicemail so I send her a text.

JESSE: *Do you want me to pick you up tonight?*

Staring at my phone, I wait for a reply but I get nothing back straightaway. I'm concerned but then again, Reese is baking to win the title tonight so I dare say, she's in competitive Reese mode and right now, I'm baking enemy number one. I look over at my snickerdoodles and smile, they aren't my best but they're still delicious.

Looking at the time, I realize I need to haul ass, otherwise I'll be late. Quickly I grab a shower and dress in jeans and an olive green Henley. My phone beeps when I'm tying my shoe laces; I hope it's Reese.

Picking up my phone, I smile when I see it is from her but I deflate when I see her short reply.

REESE: *Sure*

One word, that's all I get.

Something is up, I feel it in my bones and it's more than just the baking competition. I don't know if it's a good thing or a bad thing but I just feel that something is amiss with Reese today.

JESSE: *Great. Pick you up at 5 p.m.*

I'm tempted to add, I love you but we have yet to say that to each other. I know that I do but I'm scared to voice it. What if those three words are the end of us? My phone pings and again, she replies with one word.

REESE: *Okay*

My spidey senses are on high alert now, something's definitely up but I don't have time to think too much because it's time to leave. Grabbing my snickerdoodles, I head over to Reese's house. When I pull onto her street, she's out front waiting but she doesn't look happy, her face is void of any emotion whatsoever. And she looks tired, she's not my effervescent Short Stack and I don't like this at all.

"Hey, Jackass," she greets me, as she climbs into my Jeep. Leaning over she kisses my cheek and smiles but it feels forced. I don't like seeing her like this, she carefully rests her rum balls on her lap and when I see the care she's taking for them, a feeling of ease washes over me, she's just nervous. I remember what she was like in high school when it came to a big test, I guess this is the same, she's just nervous about the baking contest.

"Hey, Short Stack. You look stunning today," I honestly tell her as my eyes rake over her delectable body. She's wearing knee-high boots, tights, and a sweater dress that accentuates each and every curve and her tits look amazing tonight.

"Thanks," she says, again giving me a one word answer.

"Everything okay?" She nods but doesn't say anything else. "You sure?"

She turns to look at me. "I'm sure. Just nervous."

"Worried my doodles will kick your balls?"

"Pluh-ease," she scoffs, "my balls are gonna kick your doodles' ass." And for the first time since I picked her up, she smiles and it reaches her eyes. She places her hand on my knee and squeezes. "Let's go so I can officially kick your doodles' ass."

"Moving on from my balls to my doodle, are we?"

"Yep," she cheekily replies with a wink and just like that, my girl is back, but in the back of my mind, there's still a niggling feeling that something else is up.

She lifts her hand from my knee and cups my cheek in her palm, it looks like she wants to say something but her cell beeps, snapping her attention away from whatever she was going to say. She pulls away and grabs her phone. "It's Drew, she and Rusty have a table over near the funnel cake stand."

"That's an odd spot, I thought Drew would be by the bar boozing it up on rum punch, or whatever that girls' shit is that she drinks."

"For the next nine months she won't be." Reese's eyes bug wide open and she covers her mouth. "Forget what I just said."

"They're pregnant?"

"Nooooo," she draws the word out and I eye her. "Okay, yes they are, but you can't say anything."

Miming zipping my lips, I grab the fake key and slip my hand between her breasts, pocketing said key and going for a sneaky squeeze too. She smacks my hand away. "Fiend."

"Have you seen your boobs today? They're on point."

She looks down at her chest and then back up at me, worry mars her pretty face. "You're such a boob man."

"Only for yours, baby."

She rolls her eyes but that grin that I love proudly sits on her face, easing my worries from just moments ago. "Just drive, Jackass."

"Yes, ma'am," I reply with a salute. Putting the car into gear, I pull away from the curb and make my way to the fair. Parking the Jeep, we each grab our baked goods and we make our way over to where the baking competition is held. We each sign in, drop off our treats, and then head over to meet Drew and Rusty.

When we reach them, Drew is devouring a funnel cake with gusto. I'm about to tease her when I remember that I'm not meant to know so I bite my tongue and just say hello like a normal person.

Later that evening, Stefanie, this year's Christmas bake-off coordinator—much to Mom's disgust since she was also the county fair coordinator—announces, "And the winner of the annual Christmas bake fair is Reese Turner with her decadent rum balls." Everyone starts clapping, then she adds, "The ones decked in nuts sealed the deal for me."

Drew, Rusty, and I all cheer for Reese as she walks toward Mrs. Arnold to claim her ribbon. She poses for the obligatory photos and she's glowing, smiling with glee. She eventually makes her way back over to our table and takes a seat next to me.

"I knew you'd win," I tell her, placing a kiss on her ear. She shivers and I cannot wait to see her shiver while naked later this evening.

Drew joins us, she's now eating a hotdog smothered in cheese, chili, and mustard.

"That's disgusting, babe," Rusty says to his wife, but she ignores him and homes in on her gross hotdog.

Reese's face turns green and before anyone can say anything, she jumps up and races off. Looking to Drew and Rusty, they both shrug. Standing up, I follow Reese and find her bent over and throwing up.

"You okay, Short Stack?" I ask, gently rubbing her back. She lifts her head up, tears are pouring down her cheeks. "Reese, babe, what's the matter?"

She stares at me and through her tears she mumbles two words that shock the shit out of me. "I'm pregnant."

"Come again?" I say, not quite sure I heard her correctly.

"I'm pregnant, Jesse. Clearly you're a shitty bus driver because you didn't pull out to avoid children."

"I thought you were on the pill?"

"I am but clearly this falls into the point-zero-one-percent category."

Silently I stare at her, processing her words. A smile graces my face at the news and joy fills my heart, my reaction takes us both by surprise.

"You're okay with this?" she hesitantly asks me.

"Yeah, I am." I pause. "Are you?"

"I'm shocked. Scared. A little excited." She sighs and looks up at me. "To be honest, I was scared to tell you."

"Why?"

"Well, you can be a jackass—"

"I'm your Jackass and your my Short Stack."

"Not what I meant but yes, you're my Jackass and I'm your Short Stack. Are you really, really okay with this?"

"Reese, I really, really am okay with this." Sliding my arm around her waist, I pull her to me and I press my lips to hers but she pushes me away.

"Eeeeew, I have vomit mouth."

"I don't care. I want to kiss my baby momma and the woman I love."

Her eyes widen to the size of dinner plates. "You... you love me? You can't, it's too soon."

"I can and I do. Reese Turner, I love you with all my heart."

She blinks rapidly and then says four words that I

will never tire of hearing pass through her lips. "I love you too."

Resting my forehead against her, I honestly tell her. "This kid is going to be so lucky to have us as its parents."

"And I'm lucky to have conceived since I keep decking you in the balls."

"Thornton men and their balls are tough, nothing stops them from getting what they want. After all, I got you, didn't I?"

"You say such sweet things to me," she says, her face etched with the biggest smile I have ever seen.

"It's a Thornton thing, now come here and kiss me."

"With pleasure." She drapes her arms around me and kisses me with everything she has, vomit breath and all.

This is going to be the best Christmas ever, I got the girl and the best present a guy could ask for, a baby.

...six months later

"I LOVE THAT DRESS ON YOU," JESSE'S VOICE STARTLES me as I open the front door, stepping inside. "It brings out your eyes and makes your tits look amazing." He walks over to me and presses a gentle kiss on my cheek, my skin tingling at the connection.

"Such a boob man," I tease as he takes my hand in his. I follow him over to the sofa. He sits down and I snuggle into his side, leaning back I lift my legs onto the sofa and rest my palms on my growing bump. "When have I worn it before?"

"At school, last summer," he says, his voice sending shockwaves through my body.

My hormones have been running rampant the last few weeks. "It brings out the blue in your eyes, and as I said it showcases your tits perfectly and hugs your beautiful growing belly." To emphasize his point, he cups my breast and I swallow down a moan. His touch just set my already buzzing body into overdrive.

"You really are a boob man," I quietly moan, as he continues to fondle my breast.

He shrugs his shoulders and I giggle. "Babe, I just call it as I see it and you, Reese Turner, have the most gorgeous breasts I have ever seen, especially now that you're pregnant with my baby and I really really hope that these bad boys hang around after you give birth." He squeezes again and this time I moan out loud.

"You say such nice things to me."

"You're welcome," he says. "So what do you love most about me?"

"Your face." I swallow deeply, leaning my head back, I stare up at him. My breathing picks up. "I've always loved how soft this is," I say, running my fingers over the scruff on his face. "It's so much softer than I thought." I pause, biting my bottom lip. "I would very much like to feel it between my thighs as you go down on me." I swallow deeply and then add, "Right. This. Second." Pausing between each word for emphasis.

"Well, Ms. Turner." He taps my shoulder and I sit forward. He stands up and offers me his hand. Placing my palm in his, he pulls me up into a standing position, and he wraps his arm around my waist. He stares deep into my eyes and I can feel the intensity of his gaze between my thighs. "That can be arranged." He leans down and presses his lips to mine.

Pulling back, he tugs on my hand and drags me down the hallway to our bedroom—yes, OUR bedroom, Jesse moved in two weeks ago. I know it's soon, but we're about to have a baby together, that too soon boat has sailed.

We step into the room and stop at the end of the bed. "Reese, lose the dress, get on the bed, spread those legs, and I'll happily dive between your thighs. As I've always said, you have the sweetest cunt in the history of cunts."

"Must you use the 'C' word?" I admonish him with an evil eye and a scowl, still after all these years I cannot stand that word.

"Okay, let me rephrase, Reese Turner, you have the sweetest pussy in the history of pussies."

"Much better."

Placing a quick kiss on his lips, I step back and lift my hands. I begin to undo the buttons down the front of my dress. The look in his eyes right now is carnal and my body is already thrumming at what's about to happen.

What my sexy jackass doesn't know is that I'm naked underneath my dress, I removed my undergarments before I came inside just now. I've been horny all morning, waiting to get home to him. My breasts spring free, garnering a growl from Jesse. That sound causes my clit to throb and my nipples harden due to the cool air hitting the sensitive buds. He watches me intently as I continue to undo the buttons on my dress. When I reach my belly button, I slip my arms out and push the material over my hips. It flutters to the floor and I stand naked before him.

"You had nothing on underneath this?"

"Yep," I reply with a shrug. Kneeling on the edge of the mattress, I get onto all fours and crawl up to the pillows. Hoping that I look like a sexy panther and not a fat pregnant frump. Turning around, I lie on my back and spread my legs, just like he requested. His gaze drops between my thighs and his eyes bulge wide open, and his cock strains in his cargos, when he sees my bare lips, glistening with arousal.

"You shaved too?"

"Waxed," I offer. "Hurt like a mofo, but it's ohh so smooth and sensitive." With my eyes locked on him, I slide my finger down my slit.

"Uhh ah," he growls. "Mine."

Smirking at him, I shrug. "Well, have at it, Jackass."

"With fucking pleasure, Short Stack."

With my eyes locked on his, I defy him and continue to slide my finger over my sensitive nub. I close my eyes and moan, giving myself over to the pleasure coursing through my body.

He grabs my ankles and drags me to the bottom of the bed. My eyes open in surprise and a squeal breaks free, I giggle but that giggle quickly dissipates when my sexy AF man drops to his knees and lowers his head between my thighs.

"Fuuuuck," I mewl. He licks me from taint to clit, his warm tongue hits my throbbing nub and I almost come from the sensation. Ever since my wax this morning, I've been super sensitive and right now, his tongue feels like heaven. His beard tickles me and when he groans, combined with my pregnancy hormones, it heightens every nerve ending in my nether region.

He slides a finger in, and I see stars behind my eyes. "Fuuuuck!" I scream. Lifting my hands, I grip my breasts, tugging on my nipples as he continues to assault me with his mouth, tongue, and fingers.

I'm in heaven right now, orgasmic heaven.

"Jesse," I moan as he continues to ravish me. Gripping the sides of his head, I push him farther into me. "Yes," I pant, "don't stop." He nips my clit and I explode; I climax hard. Since becoming pregnant, my orgasms have been out of this world amazing and this one is no different.

He licks and sucks every last drop of my release from me. Lifting his head, his chin is coated in my juices. The liquid shimmering in the afternoon light.

Sitting up, I grip his cheeks and press my lips to his. My tongue licking along the seam, tasting myself, I moan at the flavor. "That was amazing," I murmur against his lips, before slipping my tongue inside his mouth. "I love you, now fuck me."

"Yes, ma'am." And fuck me he does.

After another earth-shattering orgasm, we collapse onto the bed completely spent. Jesse climbs off and walks into the bathroom, while I shuffle to the edge and in a very unsexy-like manner I sit up and lean back on my arms. Looking up, I see Jesse in his boxer briefs staring down at me. He cups my cheek in his palm, his eyes are full of love for me.

"Marry me?"

My eyes pop wide open and I stare up at him. "Come again?"

"Marry me, Reese?" he says stepping closer to me. "I love you, I want this baby to have two parents with the same last name. I want it all with you. Sure we've done it backward, but I don't care. I love you and I want to spend the rest of my life with you."

Rapidly I blink, processing his words. "Yes," I quietly whisper, "Yes, I'll marry you."

Rocking myself forward, I try to stand up so I can hug and kiss my fiancé but me being me, my head collides with his balls. Once again, I deck his balls. "Ohh shitballs," I say, as I lift my hand to rub and massage them better, something I've become well accustomed to doing.

"Thank God you know how to look after my balls, and you now can do it for the rest of our lives."

Jesse drops to his knees in front of me and he cements our engagement with a kiss that leaves me light-headed and breathless. "I love you, Reese Turner soon-to-be Thornton."

"And I love you and your balls, Jesse Thornton."

Oh My Fucking God, pregnant women are crazy and lucky me, I have a pregnant bridezilla. Why I pushed for us to have the wedding before the baby arrives is beyond me. We should have just went to Vegas and got hitched and then celebrated in style once our lil' man arrives. That's right, Reese and I are having a boy.

Not only are we arguing over boys' names, but we're also arguing over EVERYTHING when it comes to the nursery and the wedding. If I didn't love this woman with all my heart, I'd be out the door in a flash.

"A blue nursery for a boy is so cliche," she snarls at me as we look over paint colors in Home Depot, for what feels like the millionth time. "I want something different. Unique. Awesome."

"Yep, ah huh," I say, just to agree because at this point, she can paint a unicorn farting rainbows for all I care. We left home two hours ago, yep, for two hours we've been going through paint swatches, the colors are all starting to blur together by now. "Short Stack, just pick a freakin' color, I don't care anymore."

She snaps her head toward me and from the murderous look on her face, I know I just fucked up. "You don't care?" she screeches, and I'm sure they heard her next door in Costco. "You don't care?" she loudly repeats again. "Why am I not surprised?" she huffs. Throwing her hands up in the air, surprising me that she didn't hit my balls. "Do you even love us? Do you even want to have this baby? Get married? Do you even care?" She's crying now. "Do you even want to marry my fat, pregnant, crazy ass?"

Taking a deep breath, I hesitantly step toward my psychotic fiancée—don't you tell her I referred to her as that—and I grip her upper arms, pulling her into me, I wrap my arms around her and hug her. "Reese, babe, I love you both to the moon and back and I want to marry you more than anything an—"

"More than my pregnant boobs?"

"Weeelll,"

"Fiend," she teases, smacking me in the chest and just like that, my happy Short Stack is back, freaking pregnancy hormones are up and down like an out-of-control yo-yo.

"Is that a smile I see?" She nods. "Do you feel better after your meltdown?" She nods against my chest again. "Do you want to put the paint color selection on hold and have me take you home? I can get acquainted with the girls and then I can make love to you until you're a panting squirming mess screaming my name for everyone in town to hear?"

She lifts her face to mine and I brush away her tears. "I'd like that very much...I'm sorry I'm such a psychotic, emotional, crazy pregnant lady."

"It's okay, babe, I knew you were a psychotic, emotional crazy lady before I got you pregnant. It's one of the reasons I love you so much."

"Hardy har har, mister." She wraps her arms around me and rests her head against my chest. "That one," she says, reaching out she points to a swatch. "Slate green," she whispers. She has a huge smile on her face as she stares at the little green card.

"I love it," I tell her, and even though I would have agreed to any color right now, she actually picked the one I wanted in the beginning.

"Really?" she questions me.

"Really, really. Now pocket that swatch. I need to get my baby momma home so I can become acquainted with her tits and cu...pussy."

"Nice save there, Jackass, and it sounds like a plan." She pulls away from me and when she reaches out to grab the swatch, she bends over and screeches like a banshee.

"Short Stack, you okay?" I ask, resting my hand on her lower back. Just as I finish asking her, a pile of water gushes down her legs.

She stands upright and her eyes are wide open. "My water just broke."

"But you aren't due for another six weeks."

"Well, seems your son is an impatient bastard like

this father and wants to be here now." Her eyes widen farther. "We aren't married yet," she cries. "We need to be married before he arrives."

"Let's get you to the hospital and then we can worry about that."

"Yep. Sure. Okay," she agrees. Grabbing her hand, we turn around and start making our way out to the car. She stops suddenly and I think another contraction is here but she points to the color swathes. "Grab that green one, I don't want to forget."

"Really?"

"Just do it," she screeches and bends over, clutching her stomach as another contraction hits. I don't move, I stand next to my fiancée and let her squeeze the ever-loving shit out of my hand.

The contraction passes. "Okay get the swatch and let's go before another one comes."

Not wanting to enrage her, I grab a few of the color cards and quickly race back to her. We start walking toward the exit but she bends over again and wails. The sounds coming from her right now are unlike anything I've heard before and I've had Reese screaming many many times since we got together. They don't tell you how hard it is for the man to watch his normally strong woman screeching in utter pain while in labor. All I can do is stand by and helplessly watch. She looks up at me. "He's coming,"

"I know, babe, I'll get you to the hospital."

"No," she cries, shaking her head, "he's coming now."

"Now, now?" I ask.

"Yesssss!" she screams again, garnering attention from those around us.

"Fuck, fuck, fuck, umm, ahh, what the fuck do I do?" I ask her. I'm freaking the fuck out right now. This isn't taught in the classes so I'm out of my league right now.

"Call a fucking ambulance and then you need to deliver our son." She leans against a wall and begins to slide down. "I can't believe I'm going to give birth in Home Depot."

"At least it's not Walmart."

"Not the time for jokes, Thornton." She starts to breathe like she was taught in our Lamaze class.

"Is everything okay?" an employee asks, looking at Reese leaning on the wall panting like an elephant.

"She's about to have our baby," I tell the young kid.

"Shouldn't you do that in a hospital?"

"In a perfect scenario yes, but our lil' man has decided that he wants to make an appearance right now."

"Ohh shit, let me get the manager." He races off, leaving me with Reese.

"Do you need help?" a gentleman asks us. I look at him questioningly. "I'm a doctor. My wife and I are on a road trip passing through."

"Seriously, you're a doctor?"

"Yep, Dr. Griffin Steel." He offers me his hand.

"You two can bond later," Reese growls. "Get this kid out of me."

"Yes ma'am," Dr. Steel says. He looks to the woman with him. "Autumn, babe, can you grab my medical kit from the car?"

She nods and races away.

By now, there's quite the crowd standing around us, this is the most excitement to happen in Willows Grove, in like, forever.

"What's your name, sweetheart?"

"Reese, and this is my fiancé, Jesse."

"Nice to meet you both. Do you mind if I have a look?"

"I normally wait 'til the third date to show my bits to a man but in this instance, I guess that's fine," Reese tells him with a laugh, but before he can take a look, another contraction hits. She grabs my hand and squeezes, crushing every bone and tendon. She breathes deeply, and works her way through the contraction.

Dropping down beside her, I brush her hair off her forehead. "You're doing good, Short Stack."

"Must you fucking taunt me right now?" she screams at me as another contraction hits. "This is all your fucking fault. You and your balls are never coming near me again. I hate you right now." The contraction passes and she takes a deep calming breath. Then she pulls my hand up to her lips and kisses my palm. "I'm so sorry," she wails, "I don't mean it. I love you so much but fuck me, this hurts like a fucking bitch. I want the drugs." She looks to the doctor. "Please tell me you have all the drugs in there?"

"I'm sorry, I don't."

"No," she cries. His wife, I presume, returns and hands him his bag. She drops down beside Reese and turns her attention to her.

"I'm Autumn. You're doing good and I assure you, you're in good hands."

"You have to say that, he's your husband."

"He might be my husband, but if he was shit, I'd tell you. You're about to give birth, you need the best on hand and I promise, he's the best."

He smiles at his wife and it reminds me of how I look at Reese. "Okay, Mom, on the next contraction I need you to push."

"It's too soon," she cries, shaking her head. "I still have six weeks."

"Nope, you have about six minutes," he informs us. "Everything looks good and you're doing great. Now, hubby, slide in behind your wife and get her as comfortable as possible."

"He's not my husband yet," Reese cries. "We're getting married next weekend."

"It can be a double celebration then," Dr. Steel says.

Reese grunts through clenched teeth as I slip in behind her. She wriggles around and lies back, her head resting on my stomach. "You've got this," I whisper. She stares up at me, leaning down, I kiss her forehead and squeeze her hand reassuringly.

"I'm scared," she cries.

"Reese, you're the strongest person I know. If anyone can give birth in Home Depot, it's you."

She laughs at this and then lifts her head, staring at the doctor between her thighs with her eyes wide open. "I need to push," she growls at him.

"Okay, I need you to push with everything you have." He pauses. "Now push!" he yells encouragingly at Reese.

She clutches my hand and with everything she has,

she pushes and screams. She clamps down on my hand, lifts her head, leans forward, and continues to push.

"Once more," the doctor says.

She takes a deep breath and pushes again. Her body shakes. She grunts and groans and then the most amazing cry echoes around us. "You did it," I cry, tears welling in my eyes. "You did it, babe."

Reese collapses back and her head collides with my chest, she sighs and relaxes into me. "I did it," she reiterates just as the doctor places our little boy in her arms.

"Congrats, guys," he says, sitting back on his heels, he watches us with our son.

"Hey, baby boy, I'm your mommy and this is your daddy. Guess you couldn't wait to meet us, huh?"

I laugh at her words and stare down at the two most important people in the world and I realize, that as long as I have them, I don't care what color the nursery is, or even what we call him. I'm just happy that I get to call them mine and then I see, next to Short Stack, the color swatch.

"Slater," I voice, "let's call him Slater." Reaching down, I pick up the swatch and show her.

"Slater Thornton, I love it." She looks up at me and never has Short Stack looked more beautiful than she does right now.

"I love you."

"I love you too," I repeat. Leaning down, I press my lips to hers and Slater makes a sound in her arms. "I think he loves us too."

The paramedics finally arrive. Griffin chats with them and tells them everything that happened. Before they whisk the three of us away to the hospital, I thank Griffin for all that he did and invite him and Autumn to our ceremony next weekend.

I was looking forward to making Reese my wife and now, I can't wait for us to officially be a family. Short Stack and Slater are my everything, and I'll be sure to tell him that teasing ISN'T the way to win the girl's heart, honesty is the best policy when it comes to love.

...twenty year school reunion

"Okay, you three need to behave for Granny and Grumpy."

"They'll be fine," Jenny, the best mother-in-law in the history of mother-in-laws assures me as we drop off Slater and the twins, Kayla and Manning.

Tonight, Jesse and I are attending our twenty-year school reunion and we rented a lake house nearby so we don't have to drive home. To add to the excitement of the evening, my sneaky sneaky husband has a surprise in store for me, hence the sleepover at Da and Nanna's place tonight. "Now, say bye to Mom and Dad and then we can go find Da."

"Bye, Mom. Bye, Dad," they shout in unison and run off. No kisses or cuddles, my babies are growing up. They'll have left home before I know it and then it'll just be Jesse and me, but I don't mind at all. After all these years, I still unequivocally love my Jackass.

"Bye kids, behave," I shout into the house but they are gone, in search of their Da, who will no doubt have a sugary treat waiting for them. He's a bigger kid than Slater, Kayla, and Manning when it comes to sweets, but then again, isn't it a grandparents' prerogative to spoil their grandchildren?

"They will," Jenny assures me, "you know they will. You've raised good kids. Now, go have fun."

She winks at Jesse and my eyes widen. "She knows and I don't?" I whine.

"Maaaaybe," my husband draws out.

"Maybe my ass, this is soo unfair," I huff, crossing my arms, causing my breasts to push up in the dress that I'm wearing and the boob man that my husband is, his eyes home in on them. He licks his lips and lifts his gaze up to mine and with the heated carnal look reflecting back at me, my body begins to buzz. Our sex life is just as amazing now, as it was when we first got together and conceived our little man. Sure it wasn't smooth sailing to begin with and we kinda sorta got off on the wrong foot because he thought teasing me was the way to win my heart, but once we put our defenses away, we fell hard and fast in love. Hence why Slater was conceived so quickly but I wouldn't change a thing. He's still my Jackass and I'm still his Short Stack.

"You ready, Mrs. Thornton?" he asks, breaking the silent eye-fucking happening between us right now.

"You bet, Mr. Thornton." Turning to his mom, I

smile. "Thanks again and we'll pick the kids up around lunchtime tomorrow.

"No rush. Da and I love having them. Go and enjoy your child free night."

"We will. Just call if you need anything."

"We'll be fine, now go."

Jesse takes my hand, laces our fingers, and ushers me down to the car. We upgraded Johnny Jeep for Robbie Ram when I got pregnant with the twins, the Jeep wasn't quite big enough for a family of five.

Jesse pulls away from the curb and I turn in my seat to face him. "So, what do you have in store for me tonight, mister?"

"Wouldn't you like to know," he teases as we head toward Ryan's parents' lake house.

"Well, yeah, that's why I'm asking."

"I can't share all my secrets with you."

"What about my spousal privilege?"

"What the hell is that?" he asks me with a laugh.

"Well, as husband and wife we're meant to share everything. According to *Dr. Phil* secrets aren't good for a relationship."

"Trust me, this secret will be worth it," he replies, as we pull up outside the house next to Ryan's.

"Never trust anyone who says trust me," I huff, crossing my arms and pressing my breasts up, hoping that he will be mesmerized by the girls and spill the beans on this secret of his.

"You keep puffing your tits up like that and we won't make it to the reunion because I'll spend the night drowning in those puppies."

"You're such a fiend."

"You love it," he nonchalantly says. He leans across the center console and beckons me to him with his finger. And like a moth to a flame, I lean over to him. "I was hoping that maybe tonight, I can finally get the blowie you promised me by the lake in senior year."

"I might be able to do that...but first, you need to tell me what this big secret it?"

"You drive a hard bargain, Mrs. Thornton, bu—"

"I think it's YOU that's hard, Mr. Thornton," I tease, cupping his growing erection in my hand.

"Fuuuuuuuuck," he groans, "how about a quickie before the reunion in our house?" He places emphasis on the word our, and nods toward the house we're parked in front of. My attention is no longer on blow jobs but on the house before me.

Pulling my hand back from his dick, I stare quizzically at him. "What do you mean by OUR house?"

"Exactly that, OUR house."

My eyes widen and I excitedly squeal, "You didn't."

"I did," he replies with a nod.

"But how? Why? I don't understand."

"The night of Ryan's party in senior year, you said you wanted to own it one day."

"I mentioned that in passing, I didn't think you'd remember that."

"I remember everything about you, Short Stack."

My heart is soaring right now. "Okay, but how?"

"You know how Mr. Reynolds recently passed away?" I nod. "Well, the maintenance became too much for Mrs. Reynolds to keep up with by herself and now that it's just her, she doesn't need a five-bedroom lake-front cottage, except for when the kids and grandkids come to visit. So she popped it on the market. As soon as I found out, I put in an offer. It was accepted and as of 3:00 p.m. yesterday, we officially own it."

"You mean the house that I've lusted over forever is officially ours?"

"Yep," he says matter-of-factly.

"You are so getting that blow job by the lake tonight."

"Baby, I can get a blow job by the lake anytime I want now."

"With an attitude like that you won't." He nonchalantly shrugs but right now, he can do whatever the hell he wants because he bought my dream house. "Can we go inside before we head to the reunion?"

"We can do whatever you want, Short Stack."

We both climb out and I join him by the hood. I slide my arm around his waist and he throws his over my shoulder, pulling me to his side. He places a kiss on my head as I gaze adoringly at our new house. "Did I do good?" he asks.

"Very, very good."

Pulling away from him, I lace my fingers with his and walk around the side and down to the lake. I stop by 'the' tree and push him back against it. Reaching up, I cup his cheeks in my palms and pull his lips down to mine. We make out, against the tree, just like we did twenty years ago.

Sliding my hands down his body, I cup him through his pants and he moans into my mouth. "Really? Now? Here?" he asks against my lips. "The sun's still up."

"Yep," I reply letting the 'p' pop. "I'm finally going to take care of that," I squeeze his dick for emphasis, "by the lake for you."

"Have at it, Short Stack."

"Jackass," I cheekily reply before I drop to my knees before him. I make quick work of opening his pants, I bite my lip as I free his engorged, glistening cock.

"I love when you bite your lip like that."

"You'll like this better," I huskily say.

Opening my mouth, my tongue darts out and I gently brush it across the head of his cock. Jesse hisses and it quickly turns into a moan when I suck on the tip.

"Fuuuuuuuuck," he growls, "I love your mouth on my cock."

"Mmmhmpf," I mumble around his dick.

The moment is perfect, until from Ryan's deck we hear, "Who's getting down and dirty over there?" My eyes widen at being caught and I stumble in fright. Jesse's dick pops from my mouth and my arms flail about as I start to fall backward, trying to prevent myself from toppling over. With my arms flying about, I deck Jesse in the balls with the back of my hand.

He bends down to cup his jewels and in doing so, headbutts me, "Fuuuuck," we both shout.

I fall backward, landing on my back. Jesse trips on a root and lands on top of me with a thud.

"Ugggggh," I groan from his weight being on top of me.

He rolls off me onto his back and we lie next to one another and stare up at the afternoon sky. Turning my head toward him, I begin to laugh. This sets him off and the two of us lie here laughing our asses off.

Finally we compose ourselves but we still lie on the uneven ground and stare at one another. "Sorry I decked your balls, again."

"They're used to it," he replies with a smirk, I slap him in the arm and shake my head.

Snuggling into his side, we lie here and I stare up at OUR house and take it all in. This is mine and Jesse's relationship in a nutshell, and I wouldn't have it any other way. Now that we'll be living in my dream lake house, we can do this, minus the ball decking, anytime we want.

THE END!!!!!

Recipes
from
DECK
...The Balls

rum balls

INGREDIENTS

- 200g dark chocolate
- 1/4 cup cream
- 30g butter
- 200g chocolate cake crumb (triple choc chip muffins also works)
- 1/2 cup pecans (slightly crushed)
- rum (to your liking)
- chocolate sprinkles and/or coconut for decorating

DIRECTIONS

1. Break up chocolate and place in bowl.
2. Combine cream and butter on a small pan and stir over low heat to melt and mixture is just boiling.
3. Pour hot cream mixture over chocolate until chocolate melts and is smooth.
4. Stir in cake crumbs, pecans and rum.
5. Refrigerate so mixture firms up to make rolling easier.
6. Roll heaps teaspoons into balls and coat in chocolate sprinkles or coconut.
7. Refrigerate until hard.

Snickerdoodles

INGREDIENTS

COOKIES

- 3/4 cup white flour
- 1/4 tsp baking powder·
- 1/4 tsp salt (just under level)·
- 1/4 tsp cream of tarter (optional)·
- 1/4 tsp plus 1/8 tsp baking soda·
- 1/4 cup sugar ·
- 1/2 tsp pure vanilla extract·
- 1 and 1/2 tablespoons milk ·
- 1/4 cup butter

CINNAMON & SUGAR MIX

Equal parts cinnamon and sugard
OR
two parts sugar to one part cinnamon, depending on how cinnamon-y you want your cookies.

DIRECTIONS

1. Preheat oven to 330 F.
2. Combine dry ingredients and mix very, very well.
3. In a separate bowl, melt butter, then stir in vanilla and milk.
4. Pour dry into wet and mix again.
5. Form balls.
6. For true snickerdoodles, roll each ball in a mix of cinnamon and sugar If you want soft cookies, you'll need to get the balls very cold. (So roll the balls, cover in the cinnamon-sugar, then put in fridge until cold)
7. Cook for 9-10 minutes. They'll look way underdone when you take them out, but that's ok.

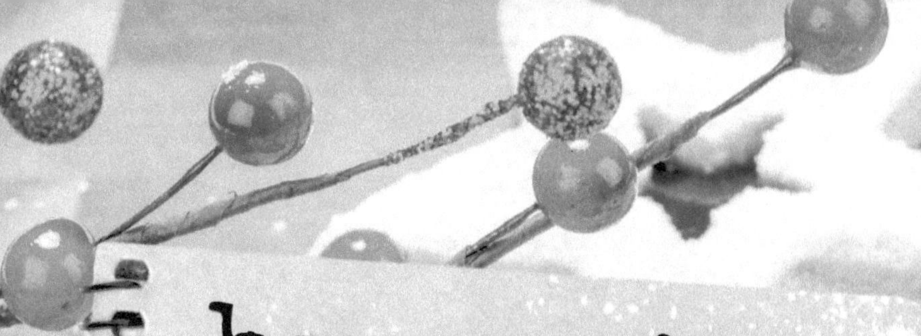

brownies

INGREDIENTS

- 200g butter
- 2 cups brown sugar
- 1/2 cup cocoa powder
- 1 teaspoon vanilla essence
- pinch of salt
- 1 cup self raising flour
- 2 eggs
- 1/2 nuts (macadamia or walnuts)

DIRECTIONS

1. Heat oven to 180º
2. Line rectangle tin with baking paper
3. Melt butter, brown sugar and cocoa powder together DO NOT BOIL
4. Take off heat and add vanilla and salt
5. Mix in flour
6. Add eggs and mix well.
7. Stir in nuts
8. Pour into tin and bake for 20-25 minutes
9. When cool, ice with chocolate or salted caramel icing

DECK…THE BALLS PLAYLIST

Wake Me Up Before You Go Go - Wham!
So What - P!nk
Summer of '69 - Bryan Adams
Calypso - Spiderbait
Cruel to be Kind - Letters to Cleo
Can't Take My Eyes off You - Frankie Valli
The Diary of Jane - Breaking Benjami
Going Under - Evanesence
I Am The Fire - Halestorm
I Hate Everything About You - Three Days Grace
Love Bites (So Do I) - Halestorm
Share Hates Me - Puddle of Mudd
(Sit-in' On) the Dock of the Bay - Otis Redding
Uptown Funk - Mark Ronson feat. Bruno Mars
American Pie - Don McLean
It's Beginning to Look a Lot Like Christmas - Michael Buble
Let It Snow, Let It Snow, Let It Snow - Dean Martin
You're Beautiful - James Blunt

Finally // Beautiful Stranger - Halsey
Need You Now - Lady A
The Gambler - Kenny Rogers
Can't Get You Out Of My Head - Kylie Minogue
Carry on Wayward Son - Kansas
I Want You To Want Me - Letters to Cleo
My Happiness - Powderfinger
Scar - Missy Higgins
Every Breaking Wave - U2
I Believe in a Thing Called Love - The Darkness
My Life Would Suck Without You - Kelly Clarkson
The Firts Cut is the Deepest - Sheryl Crowe
Hi Me With Your Best Shot - Pat Benatar
Teenage Dirtbag - Wheatus
Use Somebody - Kings of Leon
What I Like About You - The Romantics
Right Here, Right Now - Fatboy Slim

This playlist can be found on Spotify.

Want to know more about the doctor who delivered baby Slater and his wife, Autumn?
Grab your copy of Doc Steel today...and read on for a sneak peek.

PROLOGUE

...Twenty years earlier

"Are you freakin kidding me, Griff?" she shouts, her voice laced with anger, shock, and sadness. "You accept this without talking to me first?" This is not how I expected her to react. I expected excitement and happiness. Not like this.

The 'this' Autumn is referring to is I just joined the navy and entered into their medical training program. I was amazed at what they offered in regard to the training and immediately signed up. Sure, I was shocked I enlisted, it was never on my radar, but it was too good of an offer to pass up. Not only will my degree be covered by the government but they will also pay me to study. I was so excited; I accepted immediately and couldn't wait to tell Autumn the news. This will be a huge financial relief for us; the only downfall is I need to move to Portsmouth, Virginia. I was sure Autumn would be happy and excited for me. For us. I certainly didn't think she'd react like this.

"I thought I was doing the right thing," I plead, "My degree will be paid for, sure I have to serve, but in the long run, it will be great for us."

"No, Griff, it will be great for you. While you are off sailing the high seas, I'll be here. Alone." She wipes her eyes, which are now glassy with tears. "I can't believe you are going to walk away from us."

"I'm not walking away from us. I'm doing this for us. Don't you see?"

She stares at me, the first tear falls and she angrily wipes it away. "No, this is all for you."

With those words, she turns and walks away from me. Racing over to her, I grab her hand and spin her to face me. We stare at one another. Her eyes well with tears and she begins to sob uncontrollably. Lifting my hand, I wipe away her tears. Bending down, I rest my forehead against her. "Autumn, I promise this will all work out. I need you to trust me."

"I do trust you, but I just don't see how you being a million miles away will work." She swallows back a sob, "Please don't do this."

"I'm sorry, I have to."

She sighs deeply, I can finally see acceptance whirring around in her face. "When do you leave?"

My lips lift in a smile, I knew she'd come around. "In two weeks."

"What?" she screeches. "I thought we'd have more time."

"I know, me too, but now you see why I had to make this decision as quickly as I did."

She nods. "I understand," she mumbles but really she doesn't, she just said that to appease me.

"I love you, Autumn," I vow, placing a kiss on her forehead.

"I love you too, forever and eternity," she whispers back to me.

Forever and eternity, that's what we always said to one another, and I really hope that our love mantra is true.

The next two weeks, all we do is fight and bicker about anything and everything. I try everything to get her to see this is great for us. I even try to get her to come with me. She doesn't want to leave Sandpoint, it's her home. Her family and friends are here. I want her to be happy, so I stopped asking her to move with me. After a long discussion, we agree to stay together but I know we won't, there is too much hurt in her heart.

The morning I leave, she is cold and distant. I know I've already lost her. On one hand I am excited for the venture ahead, but on the other, I am losing the one I love unconditionally. We kiss goodbye but there is no passion in it, it is robotic. She stands there and watches as I walk toward the plane. The plane taking me to Portsmouth, Virginia, where I will one day become Doctor Griffin Steel.

At the top of the stairs, I look back at her and my heart broke. She is crouched down, staring at the plane, tears streaming down her face. And I know: those tears and her heartbreak are because of me. In that moment, I start to wonder if maybe I'm making a mistake...career wise, it's the best decision I ever made. In regard to Autumn; it's a huge mistake.

Grab Doc Steel today!

ACKNOWLEDGMENTS

These never get any easer to write. I'm always scared I'll forget someone, and trust me, I have before. There's so many people who tirelessly work behind the scenes to help me publish my books and without them, I would be lost. This is a blanket thank you to everyone who has ever helped me over the last seventeen books.

Now, onto the individual thank you's.

The first person, I need to thank is my cover designer, **Megan Keith** from **Designed by Grace**. Thank you for the perfect cover, again. I saw it. I fell in love with it. And I bought it. Then I annoyed you with a billion and one amendments for the full wrap and then BAM, we, well you, nailed it.

My beta babes; **Alana, Andi, Jenny, Stefanie** and **Tara** ; as always, thank you from the bottom of my heart. I'd be lost without you ladies.

Karen, my editor and friend, we did it again. Seventeen books later and we are still plugging along. Thank you for everything that you do.

Margaret, thank you for checking my I's are dotted, that my T's are crossed and that you agree with Drew's sentiment when it comes to mushrooms, those fungy F'ers DO belong back in the ground where they came from.

My family, **Troy, Piper** and **Kade;** you guys are my rock and I love you all to the moon and back.

And lastly, **you, my reader.** Thank you for once again picking up one of my books. I wouldn't be doing this without amazing readers.

Cheers
Dana **XO**

ABOUT THE AUTHOR

DL Gallie is from Queensland, Australia, but she's lived in many different places all over the world, including the UK and Canada. She currently resides in Central Queensland with her husband and two munchkins. She and her husband have been together since she was sixteen, and although they drive each other crazy at times, she couldn't imagine her life without him.

Shortly after her son was born, DL began reading again. With encouragement from her husband, she picked up the pen and started writing, and now the voices in her head won't shut up.

DL enjoys listening to music, drinking white wine in the summer, red wine in the winter, and beer all year round. She's also never been known to turn down a cocktail, especially a margarita.